PACK
NIGHTMARE

Pack Nightmare

A NEW ADULT PARANORMAL ROMANCE

MIDNIGHT WOLVES OF SMOKY FALLS BOOK TWO

LAUREL NIGHT

Chapter One

LAYLA

~

The new professor holds my gaze for several long, painful seconds before he withdraws and carries on looking around the classroom, continuing the explanation of his sudden and surprising presence.

The surrounding room is muffled; I vaguely hear Jared trying to get my attention, but it's as if he's behind a clear plastic wall. My brain dumps memories in front of my eyes in quick succession:

Derrek the first day I met him, mere hours after I ran away from foster care. Looking like a regular street kid, perhaps a bit older and wiser. Offering me a safe place to stay, taking me to what becomes my street family.

Derrek a couple years later, in a group sitting around a barrel fire, appearing absolutely perfect through the rose-colored glasses of my adoration. He looked out for me from day one, the same as he treated all the other kids. I wasn't special to him, but I liked to pretend I was. In my head every glance, every smile had meaning. I'd do anything if he asked me.

And then Derrek above me; his expression panicked while I lay on the ground. The memory is flooded with pain and confusion; the pain of course from my injuries. Confusion because, as concerned as Derrek was when he found me, I never saw him again in over a year.

Now he's turned up in Smoky Falls—practically the opposite side of the country from where I'd last seen him—and it's like he's a completely different person.

This Derrek isn't a street kid; he introduces himself as Professor Derrek Westin and he *looks* the part.

My Derrek kept his hair buzzed short, and usually had on some combination of baggy, holey jeans, with a dark t-shirt and flannel under an old, beat-up leather jacket he wore everywhere. He could pass as a regular kid from a distance, but if you looked closely, it was easy to spot the street on him. His shirts were dark to conceal the dirt, and the buzz cut wasn't perfect; it was done with an old pair of clippers owned by a 12-year-old, Chacho. Chacho's dad was a barber before they shot him in a drive-by, and Chacho ended up on the street. With us.

No, this Derrek is some kind of hipster professor 2.0 version of the Derrek I knew. Instead of jeans, he wears navy blue slacks with tan leather shoes, a skinny brown belt, and a tucked in plaid shirt with a corduroy blazer on top. His outfit is like the completely grown-up version of Milo's style, slightly more professorial and a little less edgy.

But most surprisingly he's got *hair*. No more buzz cut; it looks as if Derrek has been growing it out since I last saw him. To my shock, he has sandy-colored curls, brown at the roots but nearly white at the tips. Based on the shade of his buzz cut, I always assumed he had dark hair, like me.

Assessing him now, I can't imagine why I thought I recognized him in the hall. The man before me is nothing like the boy I knew on the street. It must have been a feeling that told me I knew this person, because it certainly wasn't his appearance.

His eyes, of course, haven't changed. They were always a brilliant shade of green, so similar to my own that we sometimes passed as siblings. Even from this distance, they stand out against his fair complexion.

"Layla!" Jared's hand grasps my shoulder and gives me a little shake, startling me into hearing his desperate whispers again. "What the hell is going on? You look like you've seen a ghost!"

I swallow thickly. "I kind of feel like I have," I whisper back. "The new professor... I knew him. On the street, in LA. What's he *doing* here?"

Jared's dark eyes narrow in suspicion and he glares down at the whiteboard, where Derrek is writing details about the upcoming reading.

My gaze travels over the other students, wondering if they're suspicious about this new professor as well.

3

But the more I look, the more I wish I hadn't. The girls are watching Derrek with moony eyes, giggling and whispering behind their hands or texting rapidly.

Glancing back at our new professor, who has now removed his jacket and rolled his sleeves up to write on the board, I understand the reaction. Of course, I'd always had a crush on the older boy I considered my savior. I'm sure a few of the other girls did, too, but we were all street kids. Skinny, hungry, and not the cleanest. Normal people didn't look twice at us, and Derrek had never acted in a way other than brotherly toward us, despite my desperate fantasies about him.

But I am no longer a skinny street kid, and neither is Derrek. He's bulked up quite a bit since I last saw him, in fact. His shoulders are broad and muscular, and even though he's still lean, he definitely fills out those blue pants well. His round butt wiggles slightly as he writes on the board, and I catch a nearby classmate filming him with her bottom lip pinched between her teeth.

A surge of jealousy rips through my chest, and I force myself to take a long, slow breath.

Whatever Derrek is doing here, I'm not sure I want to know. It can't be a coincidence, but he didn't even bother to check on me in the hospital after my attack. It was like losing my parents all over again. Seeing him now, I feel echoes of the heartbreak I tamped down for the year in LA. It *still* hurts that he never came.

"Milo and Landon are going to meet us here after class. They want to get a load of this guy," Jared whispers, tucking away his phone.

"What? Why?"

"It's weird that he turned up here, don't you think?"

"Well obviously, but I don't think he'd go through the process of becoming a Lit professor just to hurt me. Unless he makes us read Tess of the D'Urbervilles and analyze the symbolism of syphilis," I snort. "In that case, I'd definitely argue that he's out to hurt me."

"What?" Jared is mystified by my rant.

Clearly, he's never read Tess of the D'Urbervilles. If he had, he'd agree with me.

"Nothing. I just don't think he's here to hurt me."

"We'll see." Jared's tone is dark with implication, and a little thump of emotion swells my heart.

These guys, my fated mates, continue to surprise me with their concern. Perhaps I should be annoyed that they've appointed themselves my protectors, but truthfully, it's been so long since I really felt someone cared about me—Layla, as an individual—that I continue to be shocked and flattered.

Of course Derrek looked out for me, but delusions of romance aside, I knew I wasn't special. There were over twenty kids in our crew, and Derrek never treated me differently than any of the others.

But when those bright green eyes lock on mine again, I can't help thinking: *But he's not with any of those other kids now. He's here with me. That has to mean something.*

Chapter Two

LAYLA

~

Somehow I make it through all fifty minutes of the class. I take a few half-hearted photos of the whiteboard to make sure I don't miss anything important, but I'm certain there isn't a single word that leaves Derrek's lips and actually lands in my head. My mind spins uselessly through the entire period, running over everything *except* literature.

Derrek leaves a stack of stapled papers at the edge of his desk, and when he dismisses us, students file by to grab one on their way out. I don't miss the flirtatious glances of other girls as they pass my former mentor-turned-professor. He smiles kindly at them, the same smile I knew from Derrek the street kid, but his posture is professional and closed off as he waits patiently.

I know what he's waiting for.

"Gorgeous, you coming?" Jared has already packed his things and is standing at the end of our row, waiting for me to descend the steps of the lecture hall and go grab a syllabus by his side.

"Um, you go on ahead. I'll meet you guys outside. I... need to talk to him alone for a minute." I give him my best reassuring smile.

Jared's dark eyes are worried, but he nods solemnly and joins the line of students filing downstairs.

I take my time gathering my things, fidgeting with my backpack zipper until I'm the last student in the seats. Slowly I descend the steps, waiting for the guy ahead of me to get his papers and leave. Glancing toward the exit, I see all three of my fated waiting for me just outside the door with anxious expressions.

Steeling myself, I step forward and approach Derrek, who's waiting for me as the picture of casual with his hands in his pockets, leaning against the desk.

My heart pounds, and I'm not even sure why I'm nervous. In the last year I hadn't thought about him romantically at all, but his sudden appearance seems to have dredged up every teen fantasy I had of him on the streets and now brings unbearable heat to my cheeks.

His gaze softens when his eyes meet mine, and his smile widens. "Lex, I was wondering when I'd see you. I feel blessed to have you in class on my first day. You look amazing, by the way. I'm so happy to see you've recovered so well."

My heart leaps at the compliment, then swiftly

drops when I realize he's not complimenting my appearance so much as my healing.

"Thanks, and it's Layla now. I guess technically my name is Lilliana, but that's still weird to me." My hands clutch the backpack straps just beside my armpits. It's so awkward, I don't know what to do with myself. If we were on the street I'd give him a hug, or a high-five. But now, after going so long with no communication at all and then him turning up as my professor? It doesn't feel right.

"Of course, Layla. I'm still Derrek, which you already knew." Suddenly he seems like the nervous one, scratching the back of his neck and rambling. "Either way, it's great to see you."

"Yeah, quite a surprise that you turned up here, of all places. After I never saw you in LA after my attack, I didn't really expect to see you again." My voice is sharp, and my hands release my backpack to cross my chest defensively. "Why are you here? I assume you know... more about this place than I did before I first arrived." I'm honestly not sure what he knows, and without alpha compulsion to keep me from saying something wrong, I am especially careful in my choice of words.

Derrek's eyes dart to the doorway, and my three fated watching us quietly from just outside. "It's a long story, Lex. Perhaps-"

"Layla," I correct him. "Summarize." The word is almost a bark of command.

He chuckles lightly. "I see you've connected with your inner alpha. That's good."

So he *does* know I'm the alpha, and that he's landed in the middle of a pack of wolf shifters. I guess that's a good start.

"Long story shortened, I'm related to your pack seer, through a long, tenuous connection. When your uncle and his witch Maria showed up to claim you, they knew right away. Your uncle offered me a place to work here, provided I could meet his requirements."

I snort; his story is *severely* lacking. "Nice try. I may have been able to get a GED in a year, but there's no way you got an entire college education in twelve months, let alone *two* degrees. What does it take to be a professor, a master's? A PHD?"

He slips a finger between his collar and throat, clearly uncomfortable. "The truth is, I'm not as young as you probably thought I was, back in LA. I had my bachelors and started my master's before I ended up there, so I just had a couple of semesters to finish before I could legally teach."

My stomach takes a sickening flop. "How old *are* you?"

"I'll be twenty-eight next month." Derrek's expression is distinctly guilty, and his eyes drop to the ground.

The sudden pressure on my chest feels like a thousand pounds, making it difficult for me to draw breath. "You're *ten years* older than me? Jesus, Derrek, I... don't know what to say. What the hell were you doing, running around with a bunch of homeless teenagers on the street, living under a fucking bridge, when you already graduated and even had a degree? Surely there were more options for you than there were for the rest of us."

His voice is soft. "They needed me." He raises his face to look at me directly, eyes blazing with sincerity. "*You* needed me."

I'm taken aback by his statement, but my inner voice tells me there's nothing but truth here. I shake my head, mentally calculating. "That still makes *no* fucking sense. If you wanted to help street kids, at twenty-four you could have volunteered at a shelter, or that soup kitchen we sometimes visited. I bet there were lots of ways for a college-educated *man* to help troubled teens. Boys and girls' club. None of them involve pretending to be younger than you were, choosing to be homeless."

Derrek's gaze sharpens. "But you couldn't be in the boys and girls' club, could you? Because you were a foster care runaway, Lex. In order to get that kind of help, you had to be in the system. Same as those other kids. So no, volunteering for those organizations wouldn't have done the same thing, because it wouldn't have helped you or the others."

"It's Layla, and how exactly did you help: by turning us into better thieves?" I spit. It's a low blow, but I'm furious. I feel so *stupid*. While he's still young and handsome, it's obvious now that he's much older than I'd assumed. Did he ever tell me an age, or did he just allow me to believe what I wanted to believe? I can't remember now.

"You know I did more than that, *Layla*. I kept the pimps and the gangs away from a rag-tag group of street kids for over four years. I protected you, all of you. I kept Chacho from joining the 76th Street Killers, for one. I gave him an option other than falling into gang life to get by." His tone softens abruptly. "You might like to know, I finally got him to go into foster care. He was adopted last month, actually. By a really great family."

My heart lurches—Chacho was such a mouthy little wannabe gang-banger in huge jeans and stained white tank tops. Derrek paid him for his questionable haircuts because the kid had a strong sense of pride; he wouldn't do the community sharing the rest of us took part in. He wanted to pay for everything he received. It almost brings tears to my eyes to imagine him, cleaned up and wearing an actual shirt, sitting down to a family dinner with kind people.

"And what are the rest of them doing, now that you're not there to 'protect them' anymore?" I can't help myself from digging for something to be angry about. It's like an intense need I have no control over.

"Well, you might not realize this, but a lot of them are technically adults now. After you left, I started working on getting them into the system, getting aid and housing, educations. The younger ones I worked on, a few went into the system and ended up in good places—yes, I checked up on them," he cuts off my angry protest. "There are still a few that refused, and I left Hendrix in charge. You remember Hendrix, I'm sure."

The kid who went by Hendrix was always quieter than most of the others. More than once I'd spotted him in the library, spending his days reading and enjoying the free air conditioning much like I did. He never got into fights with other kids, but I'd seen him stand up for a smaller kid being bullied by an older one when Derrek wasn't there to keep the peace. Hendrix was a good choice for leader.

I sigh. "Well, I'm glad to hear that some of them are in better spots than they were a year ago. And yes, I remember Hendrix."

"Do you approve?" Derrek lifts an eyebrow, a smile tugging at the corner of his lips.

"It still doesn't make sense to me. If you went that far, if you were so determined to protect all those kids, how could you just walk away like that? But yes, I think Hendrix was a good choice, and I'm glad Chacho and some others have actual homes now."

He nods. "Me too. It's strange to be here with you, in such a different setting. But I was always sort of a mentor—or at least I tried—so I hope the adjustment time is minimal. From the sounds of it, you've been through a lot since I last saw you."

"I'll say." My hurt feelings resurface after the reminder. "I suppose I'm lucky I had someone to take care of me, since none of my *friends* bothered to show up once the ambulance took me away."

Derrek's eyes narrow, and he stands, straightening to his full six feet. "Is that what they told you? We sat *all night* in the ER. Me, and several of the others. They wouldn't let us in since we weren't family. I didn't leave the hospital for two days, and when your uncle showed up, they said you were being moved and wouldn't tell me where. I made such a scene he came to talk to me himself, and that's when he figured out who I was." He pauses to fish a brown leather wallet out of his pocket and pulls out a somewhat battered business card. I turn it over, seeing my uncle's name and the city crest of Smoky Falls, along with contact information.

"He gave me this, told me to call him. I assumed once they had you stabilized he'd invite me to come visit in Smoky Falls, but he just gave me a list of requirements and said they could get me a position at SFC if I finished my master's. He must have researched me. I have no idea how he knew so much."

My heart thumps painfully. "Derrek, I was in LA for a *year*. I just got to Smoky Falls in time to start the semester. Two *months* ago."

Derrek's shock is genuine. "Are you kidding me? You're fucking with me, right? There's no way. They said..." he trails off, thinking.

"Did they actually say I was in Tennessee?" My voice is hard, and I'm ready to whip my phone out and bitch Roxanne out right now if they lied to him.

"No, I don't remember them saying it directly. It was just implied. I knew they were moving you, so I guess I

14

just assumed." He sighs, visibly deflating. "Where were you?"

"They moved me to Cedars Sinai, and when I recovered, I was in an apartment nearby so I could get my GED and attend physical therapy. My arms were pretty bad," I admit.

"I'm so sorry, Lex- Layla. I promise if I'd known you were in town, I'd have come to visit. We *all* would have. But... you never came back, either." His statement isn't an admonishment, just an implied question.

I swallow, my mind racing. I don't know how much he knows about the pack; we haven't really discussed it in detail.

"I... wasn't allowed to go back," I answer finally, which is true. "They were worried the person who attacked me might try it again."

Derrek's eyes darken. "I suppose that's fair."

"Did they ever catch the guy? Or know what he was after?"

"They never made an arrest." His gaze darts away, a guilty expression crossing his face.

"I see."

Silence falls over us, and I've run out of anger. I still feel like he's not telling me the whole truth, but I don't know how to process it. He's not part of the pack, so I can't feel him the way I feel the others.

Still, there's something there. Something about him that's different from normal humans. Tourists visiting town on the weekend are different, and I've gotten good at recognizing pack as separate from normies.

Now I have a third category—something else. This sense must be how my uncle knew Derrek belonged here. I try to think back to my visit to the pack seer and remember if this is how it felt to be around her, but I was so revved up after the fight, I truthfully don't recall. I'll have to ask Roxanne about it.

"Hey Layla, everything okay?" Landon's worried voice carries into the classroom and I jump away from Derrek guiltily. Even though we weren't doing anything, it somehow feels like a small betrayal to be here alone with this man, on whom I had a burning crush for years, when I have three fated mates waiting for me just outside.

I turn to see the three of them filing into the classroom, all staring at Derrek with suspicious eyes. A small smirk curls my lips; I guess they were tired of waiting.

"Yeah, I was just catching up with an *old friend*," I say, my voice thick with implication. "Guys, this is Derrek, we were friends in LA. He was sort of the leader of our pack of runaways. Derrek, this is Jared, Landon, and Milo." I gesture to each of them as I say their names, watching them subtly trying to look bigger. Derrek's obviously an older guy, and they clearly feel somewhat territorial about me, but I'm not sure what puffing up their chests is supposed to achieve.

"Yeah, Jared told us." Milo steps forward and offers Derrek his hand, his blue eyes cool and assessing. "Nice to meet you, Derrek."

The older man smiles and accepts the shake. "Likewise."

After two more begrudging handshakes, the guys seem to have lost their patience for the afternoon. "Lex, are you ready to go? We want to get out of here before Jared's coach catches him skipping practice." Milo gives me his signature half-smile, and a scowl crosses Jared's face.

"He's probably going to make me run laps tomorrow. But an afternoon off with Layla is worth it." Jared's dark tone turns sweet, and he gazes at me with a wide smile.

"Nah, Lex can have Roxanne text the coach and say she needs him. He won't question the beta."

Derrek glances my way with amusement lighting his eyes. "So he gets to call you Lex, but I don't?"

Heat warms my cheeks again. "I kind of introduced myself to him as Lex out of habit, but everyone else knows me as Layla. I can't seem to break him of it now."

"Well, I'd say if anyone has a right to call you Lex out of habit, that would be me. Since I've known you the longest."

I would swear his tone is almost flirtatious, except he's never been remotely flirtatious with me before, and I'd hardly expect him to start now. I might guess he's trying to goad the boys, get under their skin a little, but I can't imagine why.

Derrek glances casually at Milo, who glares at him

in response. "Only if it's okay with you, of course," he adds, returning his gaze to me.

"Um, whatever, it's fine. Guys, let's go. Derrek, I guess... I'll see you Wednesday."

"Not if I see you first, Lex," he replies with a wink.

Chapter Three

LAYLA

~

"I don't like him." Jared's expression is fierce, his dark brows flat below the brim of his baseball cap as he glares out the windshield on our way to Harridan House.

"Me either," Landon agrees from the back seat of the pickup.

"Same." Milo adds.

I can't help the snort of a laugh that escapes me. "Wow, who would have predicted that one?"

"What do you mean?" Landon's tone is wounded, as if I've genuinely hurt his feelings.

I soften, just a little. I wasn't trying to hurt him. "Just that I'm not surprised my fated would dislike an older guy who suddenly shows up in my life again out of nowhere."

"Hey, that's not what this is," Milo protests. "There's something off about him, something I can't put my finger on."

"He's not *pack*," Jared states. "That's enough for me."

"Well, he said my uncle discovered he's related to the pack seer. So doesn't that, in a way, make him pack?"

Milo snorts. "No. Half the seers in the country are related in some way. Those bloodlines go a looooooong way back."

"Dom brought him here, and he knows Roxanne. So there has to be a reason. Maybe she can fill us in."

"Speaking of, can you send that message and get me out of trouble with Coach, please?" Jared's voice takes on a pleading tone, prompting me to act.

I shoot a message to Roxanne, and she responds almost immediately. "Done. But she said she won't cover for you the next time you decide to play hooky."

"Works for me," Jared replies with a wink.

I dash off another text to Roxanne about our new Lit professor and wanting to discuss it with her, and the reply takes longer to come in. "Huh. Apparently Roxanne has some functions to attend tonight, so she doesn't have time to chat with me about Derrek."

"If it's important, just order her." Milo's tone is matter-of-fact, as if I should know this. "You're the alpha, after all. Use the alpha command. I thought she serves you?"

"Well, I don't think it works over text message, but… you're right. If I'm the alpha, things should be on my schedule. Besides, if she's attending important functions, shouldn't I attend, or at least know about them?" My indignation up, I text her back, saying as much with a slightly more respectful tone.

Roxanne's reply is curt; she'll meet me in the office as soon as I arrive at home.

Once I tell the guys about her response, Jared's expression turns mischievous. "Well, if you're going to have an alpha meeting as soon as we get home, I suppose we ought to discuss this now."

My eyes dart to him curiously. "Discuss what?"

Landon pipes up from the back seat. "Homecoming!"

"Homecoming?" I echo. "Isn't that, like, a high school thing?"

"Yes and no," Milo answers. "It is a high school thing, but it's also a college thing. Typically, it's when alums of the school come back for a game with some big rival, and the school hosts a weekend of events. Since people in Smoky Falls never leave, it's sort of a big community festival."

"Oh, well, that's cool I guess." It's interesting, but not much. Unless… "Is there some special thing that I'm supposed to do, as alpha or something?"

"You probably have some hands to shake and babies to kiss, but most importantly-"

Jared cuts Landon off. "There's a dance!"

I blink twice at him, confused. "A dance? Like a square dance?"

He barks a laugh. "No, like a *homecoming* dance. Normal colleges have fraternities that host formals, but we don't have any Greek organizations, for obvious reasons. Since we're a small town and even smaller college, SFC puts on a dance every year for homecoming."

"It's really nice, at least based on the photos I've seen." Landon picks back up. "They have it at the community center, and the town goes all out. I think it's part of the way they make up for the fact that we're all stuck here."

"But didn't you guys have dances in high school?" I'm honestly confused—don't boys *hate* school dances?

"We did, but they weren't very fun. Everyone goes with their fated, and those that don't have a fated are quick to pair up with each other."

"… and since you three had a fated, but I wasn't here, you had no one to go with," I finish for him with a guilty pang in my chest. I know it's not my fault, but I feel terrible they missed out on so much just because I didn't even know about this place. Obviously, I would have loved to be here attending fancy dances instead of sleeping under a bridge.

"Pretty much," Milo agrees. "We went to prom freshman year and then decided we would not subject ourselves to that again."

"Which means that we all get to experience this

together for the first time!" Jared grins. "Since you never got to go to dances, and we didn't really either, this seems like a great way for us to make up for lost time."

"But it's more than just a dance." Milo draws my attention back to the rear seat. "Like I was saying earlier, it's an entire fall festival. There's a marketplace in town, hayrides, and of course the football game. Then the dance is the next night."

"So, when is this all happening?" I ask, confused. "And why haven't I heard anything about it?"

Jared sounds slightly apprehensive. "Well, there're posters and stuff up all over campus. I'm sure you've seen one. But we didn't bring it up because you had so much on your plate already with the alpha challenge. Now that we're past that, we figured it was time to make plans."

"You still haven't told me when this is," I remind him.

"It's in two weeks, the last weekend in September. Well, really it's more like a week and a half, since today is Monday and it starts Thursday next week, with the dance on Saturday."

"Two weeks? That's hardly enough time to plan for all of this... isn't it?" Not having attended a formal dance ever, I really have no idea what is or isn't enough time. But movies always make it seem like something people plan for months.

Jared just laughs. "I'd be willing to bet my auntie has already made most of the arrangements. I don't think we need to go out to eat anywhere, unless you want to? There's no better chef in town than William, and the alpha usually hosts a dinner party in the formal dining room on Homecoming, so we can all just eat here, then go into town for the dance."

"Oh. Well, I suppose that makes it simple." Knowing Roxanne, she's already picked out my dress and shoes. It's probably waiting for me in my closet and I didn't even notice. "I guess I'll ask her about that at our little meeting today."

We pass through the security gate with ease, pull up to Harridan House, and I hesitate before hopping out of Jared's enormous pickup.

"Is there anything else coming up that I should know about? Any other alpha traditions or town festivals?"

"Well, there is this one tradition you should probably know about," Jared says seriously, and my anxiety revs up slightly. "It happens every year on the last day of October. Everyone goes outside at night and-"

"Let me guess, shifts into wolves and runs in the moonlight?" I interrupt, only half joking. That's sort of how I imagine the punchline of every joke at this point.

"No." Jared's face is solemn, and an irrational tingle of concern crawls over my skin.

"What is it?"

His thick lips split and curve into a bright smile. "It's Halloween, of course!"

"Oh my god, you jerk," I swat him on the arm as he doubles over laughing, and the other two cackle like hyenas in the back seat. "Seriously? I thought it was another crazy wolf thing."

"That was too easy, gorgeous. You've got to stop taking everything so seriously."

"Yeah, well, if you guys stopped surprising me with wolves and alphas and challenges and curses every day, maybe eventually I'll calm down."

"Fair enough. But I think you've gotten most of them at this point, if I'm honest."

I regard him with narrowed eyes for a moment, then lift a brow. "Are you sure?"

"Scout's honor," he replies, lifting three fingers and crossing his heart with his other hand.

"Jared, you ass. You were never a boy scout." Landon swats his head from the back seat.

"Hey, I figured it got the point across," the other boy answers, adjusting his cap. "But let's not keep my auntie waiting any longer. Miss Layla has some alpha duties to attend to."

Sighing, I push open the door and hop down. Despite my earlier indignation at being left out, something tells me I don't *really* want to know all the little details that need tending in my duties as alpha, at least not yet.

But all the same, I need to learn.

Chapter Four

LAYLA

~

The guys escort me up to the office, giving Roxanne their greetings before scuttling away to my suite to play video games. Roxanne was seated behind the desk when I arrived, but as soon as I walk through the door she stands up, grabbing a stack of papers and moving to one of the seats facing the desk instead.

I hesitate, eyeing the intimidatingly large furniture before letting my eyes drift to the chair beside her.

"The desk belongs to the alpha," Roxanne seems to take pity on my indecision. "But you don't have to sit there if you don't want to." She crosses her legs, one ballet flat wiggling in the air lightly as she waits for me to decide.

Shoring up my nerves, I choose the wing-backed

chair beside her and tuck one leg under my body. "I don't want to seem disrespectful," I begin. "I know there's a lot that you manage on my behalf, and I'm very grateful. I just think that if I'm supposed to be taking over as alpha, I should at least have some idea of what's going on."

Roxanne's dark eyes drop to her folded hands, their warm brown a stark contrast against her snowy-white blouse. "No, you're absolutely right. You should, and I apologize. I was trying to give you space to be a regular kid—it's hard enough having a full course of college classes. Besides, I'm on autopilot, just managing things as they come up." Her gaze rises to meet my eyes. "When your uncle was here, I reported to him daily and he would pick which things he'd attend to personally and which he wanted me to handle. We should start having daily meetings as well, although perhaps we can do them after school, to prepare for the following day, instead of in the morning at breakfast? I think that would be better for your schedule. "

"Yes, I think that's a great idea."

"Perhaps it's a good idea for you to take over a few tasks every week? Just small ones, so people get used to seeing you."

Dread drops in my stomach like a stone. "Is that really a good idea? I mean, I'm new here, and I'm only eighteen…"

"There have been younger alphas, and the age doesn't matter so much as the command. Now that you have your command voice, you can compel people to drop their petty differences and get along, if need be. The threat of being forced to comply always seems to help people find a resolution they can live with."

"Do you have to use compulsion a lot?" My mind drifts back to my uncle, complaining about how much energy he spent keeping the pack together.

Roxanne seems to follow my thoughts. "Your uncle's time as alpha was... fraught with issues. Most of them were really not his fault, and he did the best he could. But lack of strong leadership puts everyone on edge, and since he didn't have a fated and wasn't producing heirs, the fears about the future of the pack were rampant. I'm happy to report now that things have settled quite a bit. Without needing to keep the pack from telling you about us, there's hardly anything to compel. People are happier than they've been for almost two decades." Roxanne seems genuinely pleased to report this information, and I relax.

"I really appreciate how much you're handling on my behalf. I just want to get a better understanding of everything that goes into running this pack. Maybe we should start there, and you can make some suggestions on ways I can contribute."

Roxanne's expression softens and warms. "Of course. Shall we get started?"

By the time we go over the schedule for the week, my brain feels likely to explode. There's hardly a thing that happens in town that doesn't pass the alpha's desk. From requests to open businesses to municipal complaints, even down to neighbor disputes. It takes a while before I realize why.

"Roxanne, there's no police station here, is there? No city council, either?"

"That's correct." She nods her head, pulling her long black braids over one shoulder. "The town has a volunteer fire department, and we have a few safety officers, but they mainly just call in the alpha as needed. Since I have beta command, I'm able to resolve most disputes on your behalf until you're ready to take that duty over. Most of the pack understands that you're still new, and young, and attending school. They don't expect you to have the full reins yet."

"So what happens when visitors, normies, do something they're not supposed to do?"

"We call in the county sheriff's deputies. They have no jurisdiction in town based on our city codes, so our safety officers collect any trouble makers and bring them to the city limits for the sheriff to book. But that's pretty rare."

I nod slowly, taking it all in. "How does the alpha ensure all the decisions they make are what's best for the pack?"

A small smile forms on Roxanne's plush lips. "Well, that's the trick, isn't it? On one hand, alphas are born leaders, and their ability to manage the pack with the alpha command as well as connect with pack members enables them—you, that is—to feel out their emotions and determine a course of action that would please the most. The pack knows it's imperative to keep pack harmony. Even if they don't get their way in a dispute this time, they know grudges aren't allowed in the pack. And perhaps the next time, it'll work out in their favor."

"Well, that doesn't really tell me much," I snort. "So I just... *decide* and people are cool with it, knowing that if they don't win this time, they might win next time?"

"It's hard to explain, but you've seen a lot of things in the last six weeks that are rather difficult to explain, Layla. Trust me when I say your instincts as an alpha will guide you toward the right decision. That's the most I can give you right now."

"The only instinct I have right now is telling me you're doing a great job managing these things on my behalf, and I should continue to trust that you will let me know if something comes up that needs my direct involvement."

"That would be a wise decision," Roxanne replies with another smile.

I smile back, then sigh. "I have something else entirely to discuss with you."

Instantly, Roxanne's expression is serious. "Go ahead."

"Today I walked into class, and my old Lit professor is gone, replaced by some guy I knew in LA. Not only is he *years* older than I believed at the time, but he's not a runaway like he pretended to be those years I was on the street with him. Can you explain any of this?"

Roxanne sighs. "Truthfully, I don't know much. Your uncle met him that night in the ER when he came to claim you. Between his alpha instincts and Maria's magic, they knew he was not a regular human. I'm not sure how he figured it out, but Dom told me at that point Derrek was a distant relative of our seer, and that he would relocate here in the future. He set all the orders in motion before he left, so no one consulted me to let me know Derrek had arrived. I would have notified you if I knew."

"Okay, that was part of what was bothering me," I admit. "If I'm supposed to be alpha, I should know what's going on. Are there any other surprises of this type out there waiting for me?"

"This is the only one I'm aware of. It was a rather special circumstance."

"Yeah, I get that. But is this why you didn't let me go back?"

"I told you-"

"I know what you told me, but it always seems like there's important information left out in these 'explanations.'" My tone is sharper than I intended, but Roxanne doesn't flinch.

"What I told you *was* true. We were primarily concerned that your attacker might still be around, and that it was dangerous for you to return. However, after divulging his lineage to the boy, your uncle didn't want you to see him again until you already knew the truth about who *you* were. He was worried Derrek would let something slip, since he wasn't under Dom's alpha command. At least, that's what he told me; I didn't actually have much to do with that situation."

"So, there's nothing to his sudden appearance here other than his relationship to the pack seer and an inexplicable degree in English Lit?"

"As far as I'm aware, no. The seer has no descendants, so it's an opportunity to see if Derrek can tap into those abilities and take over the position when she dies. They're set to begin training once he settles in. It's remarkable that the two of you found each other on the street, so far from home, with neither of you knowing who you were. One might almost call it fate."

"Yeah, well, I dunno about fate, but it certainly is interesting."

"Fair enough."

Sighing, I tip my head back on the chair. "This is just all so much. I feel like I'm drowning in all the stuff coming at me with no way to turn down the flow."

"You're not drowning, Layla. In fact, you're doing remarkably well. It's probably going to feel like a lot for a while, but that's why you have me, and Mr. Carson, and Mrs. Dowling, and all the other people dedicated to your success. Including your fated. We're here to help you, and you'll catch up in time, I promise."

"Speaking of catching up," I lean forward, watching Roxanne's expression turn serious again when she sees my face. "Talk to me about homecoming."

Roxanne grins in response, her dark eyes sparkling. "Ah, I wondered when you'd bring that up. You'll be pleased to know most of the arrangements have already been made. I know your fated are excited to share it with you. We'll host a dinner—I have a guest list for you to approve and you're welcome to add to it if you like. Maxwell will drive you all there and back. It should be a fun time for you. A chance to cut loose and just be eighteen." Roxanne's eyes sparkle with excitement, almost as if she's looking forward to the event herself.

I can't help but play it up a bit more. "Sure, but you're not telling me the most important part: what am I going to *wear*?" I make my tone high and reedy, my best impression of a whiny teenager, and it draws a laugh from Roxanne.

"That is certainly not something I *ever* thought I'd hear from Layla Harridan," she chuckles. "Quite honestly, I'm shocked you're already thinking about it. Perhaps I'm finally rubbing off on you."

I snort. "Roxanne, although you seem to enjoy buying me sparkly things, I've never seen you wear anything but this uniform of button-down shirts and ballet flats. What exactly do you think would rub off on me?"

"Girl, just because I don't wear flashy outfits for work doesn't mean I don't like sparkly things. You've never seen my closet, so don't go assuming you know all there is to know about me."

My jaw drops. "Are you kidding me? This is *all* you wore in LA. For a year!"

"Yes, and I was working that entire time." The matter-of-fact statement knocks the breath from my lungs and I deflate just a little.

"Ouch," I sniff. "That was harsh." I'd considered

that time to be a little more personal than just an extremely long work shift.

Her tone softens. "You know I enjoyed spending time with you. I just meant I wasn't there to go out and party. I had to stay focused on the mission at hand, or risk losing everything."

"I'm sure you had it pretty rough, considering you couldn't shift while you were there. Was that hard?"

"Extremely. You remember I took several weekends off, and Maria would come stay with you?" I nod. "That was just me going home to run with the pack. I needed the time to shift and reconnect. I'm not the only one it was difficult for. It was a big deal for your uncle, *huge*, to have me gone for that long. Without his beta for a year, I left him with all the day-to-day work to manage on his own. But staying with you in LA needed to be done, and there was no one else he would trust with the job. It was the most important thing he ever asked of me." Her gaze softens. "It was hard, but it was a hundred percent worth it, because you're here now."

Something warm unfurls in my chest, and the tightness in my body eases. "I understand."

"So," she glances down at the notebook on her lap. "I think we have this week's events covered, and I'll let you know if anything else comes up during our daily briefs. Is there anything else you want to discuss?"

"I think that's it for now. I'd tell Chef to assume the guys are staying for dinner. It feels like they're here more than their own homes, at this point."

Roxanne nods sagely. "That's to be expected. As

your fated, their duty is to be your protectors, your supporters. If they didn't want to be around you as much as possible, we'd have to question why. As it stands, they are welcome whenever you want them here. Chef is always happy to accommodate a few extra plates at dinner."

Chapter Five

LAYLA

~

Dinner and video games are fun, but eventually the guys have to get home. In the wake of all the wolf fight practices and finally winning the alpha challenge, I made them promise we'll take a few nights off the midnight runs so we could all catch up on our sleep.

I'm not about to sacrifice that extra rest so they can stay up just as late on the new PlayStation Roxanne got me.

Regardless, I'm strangely restless after they're gone. I reach out with my feelings, and sense their warm, glowing happiness among the pack in town. When I close my eyes, it's like a color map of emotions within my head, and I can see the general contentment, like a sea of bright blue, that floats over the population.

Brighter yellow specks of discomfort or red anger are few, and seem to fade quickly as I watch. The deeper blues and purples, which I associate with happiness and peace, likely people who are relaxing, make up a large swath.

A sense of peace fills my chest, knowing that the pack is generally at ease and content.

So what is making it impossible for me to relax?

My mind drifts to Derrek, and I pluck the thread of discomfort in my heart that appears when I think of him. But it's like sending a signal out to space—my emotion doesn't connect with him the same way it does with my fated. Even so, I still feel myself connected to him in a way that is frustratingly undeniable.

Restless, I decide to visit the library and see if there's any information I can find on his history. If he's connected to our pack seer, and they're an integral part of the pack, there has to be something about his family here.

I pad into the large burgundy room and breathe in the scent of so many books. It's an intangible yet over-whelming feeling of possibility, of promise. So many pages I've not yet flipped, so many things to learn.

Over the weekend, Mr. Carson mentioned that the second floor is where more pointed materials on the pack history are shelved—that way they're out of reach for basic perusers of books, and if he wants to prevent access, he simply removes the ladder.

Tonight it's hooked on the rails, waiting for me to climb. I give the polished mahogany a shake, but it's firmly set, with locking mechanisms on the floor wheels already engaged. After a couple of tentative steps, I'm reassured by its stability, and I climb up to the mezzanine.

It's not a proper floor, just a narrow catwalk with an ornate railing and a ladder of its own to reach books on the highest shelves. Once I verify the smaller ladder is equally sturdy, I slide it to my desired stack and engage the wheel locks, then climb to the section Mr. Carson recommended. There are several books without writing on the spine that I open to discover are filled with hand-written accounts. Diaries, for a lack of a better word. The inside covers have labels added, with the name and dates of the events covered within. I flip through several, trying to read the ornate, flowing script that fills the pages.

"Ahem." Mr. Carson clears his throat and I jump so abruptly that I almost fall from the ladder. I drop the book I was looking at, and my gaze darts guiltily at Mr. Carson.

"My apologies, Layla. I waited for you to notice me, but after a period, I thought I ought to just make you aware of my presence."

"No, it's fine. I was definitely lost to the world." I descend the ladder and retrieve the small book I dropped, checking its faded green cover for damage.

"Is there something in particular you're looking for? I might be of assistance."

"That would be helpful, thank you. I just didn't want to disturb you at this hour."

"It's not a problem, Layla," he answers gruffly. "Any time of the day or night, we are here to serve you."

I gaze down at him apprehensively from the mezzanine. I'm not sure I can see myself pounding on his door well after bedtime for information. It's still nice of him to offer.

Finally descending the ground floor ladder, I can look at him directly. "I would appreciate your help. There is a new arrival in town, and the apparent story is that he's distantly related to the pack seer, and somehow Uncle Dom and Maria, the witch that helped with my recovery in LA, figured this out and invited him here to teach English Lit of all things. So I just thought I'd try to get a better understanding of the seer's role in the pack, where they came from, and how this all factors together."

Without answering, Mr. Carson gestures for the book in my hands, and I hold it out for him. He glances at it briefly, then returns it. "Lilliana Harridan the seventh, age 16, year 1902. This, while interesting, is mostly her ruminating about her fated and if she thinks they're 'cute'. It won't be of much use for answering your questions."

A hot flush creeps up my cheeks. I hadn't been able to decipher the ornate writing. I just saw the dates and thought there might be something of interest. "Okay, can you make a recommendation of which books might help?"

Mr. Carson clears his throat. "I think the best thing

to do would be to retrieve a tea service from the kitchens. I'll return momentarily."

"I don't understand. Why do I need tea to find a book?"

"I believe I can answer most of your questions, but my throat is rather dry. If we're going to sit and have a chat, I think tea, and perhaps some cookies, would be nice."

Mr. Carson lights a fire in the library first, then leaves and returns twenty minutes later with a tray of tea, small sandwiches, and cookies for two.

Now that I've been here a while, I know better than to interrupt his process as he pours and serves the tea with precision. He assures me it's caffeine-free before handing me the cup and saucer.

I'm practically quivering with impatience but there is no rushing the older gentleman, so I accept my tea and nibble a spiced cookie while he fixes his cup. After helping himself to a sandwich and a sip, he finally begins.

"In order to explain how we got here, I think you ought to know how all of this came to be. How much do you know about the origins of the pack?"

I think back on what the guys and Roxanne told me. "Just that the original shifters traveled here from the Old World, and witches helped them find the same earth magic that protected them there. They used the alpha's blood at the time to create a safe place and that is how the Harridan line got tied in to being the eternal alphas. Oh, and that there was a curse, when some of the pack split off. That's why we're all stuck here."

"Yes, that's the basics, but it's far more nuanced, I'm afraid. As these things are." Mr. Carson takes a long sip of his tea, and I bite back the leading questions I want to throw at him.

"The Old World was filled with magic. It sustained our ancestors wherever they went, connected to every rock and tree and living thing. The shifters lived as one with nature, and it supported and protected them.

As people stepped away from nature, magic began to seep out of our world. Large villages became towns, and the more unnatural things that grew, the less magic there was to go around. Almost as if the earth were withdrawing her gift from those who were unworthy. Towns turned into cities, and shifters fled to the furthest reaches of the wilderness to stay in contact with the magic.

When there was no longer a reprieve, when magic seemed to disappear everywhere, a particularly gifted witch had a proposal: she believed she could form a connection with the earth magic, forging a sacred place that would be protected from this withdrawal of magic. The packs were willing to try anything, so they hired her to cast her spell.

And it worked. Enclaves of magic started popping up across the Old World, and packs brought on witches as permanent members of the pack. Understand, at this point, we were all in it together; there was no animosity between packs. It was all shifters set on the preservation of our kind. So we all shared this knowledge. The witches worked together, helping to connect with the magic. But it became more and more difficult to maintain, and every time a witch passed, her spell faded—we had to have a new witch on hand to cast a new spell, and each time it was a little weaker than before.

Once the New World was discovered, the packs believed this was the solution they'd prayed for. Several packs remained in the Old World, afraid to risk everything they clung to on a chance there may be something better. But many opted for the risk.

It was hard going, and they suffered on the journey. There was no chance of shifting on the crowded boats, and no earth magic to connect to. At that time, the consequences weren't as dire… well, I'm getting ahead of myself.

The settlers landed and immediately set out to find the sort of sanctuary they craved. And the New World was rich with magic—they were ecstatic to set foot on the earth and feel it all around them. Mind you, these people had only known protected areas of magic, not the wild and rampant magic that lived in untamed worlds.

So they took it upon themselves to become explorers, and search for the most magical places. The witches developed stronger spells, and they had a plan: Find the places where the magic was most powerful, and preserve it immediately, before industry started the inevitable leeching of magic.

The witches were vested in the process as well; their magic was most powerful when tapped into earth magic. They could make some potions, work some small amount of magic without it. But it was more like parlor tricks than the sort of magic they could do, given the right circumstances.

As teams, the witches and the packs started on the east coast of the new world and pushed ever deeper into the wilderness. Packs might establish a sanctuary, but when it became overrun with normal humans, they moved on.

Eventually, that led further and further west, and that is how we became the Smoky Falls Pack. This place was the most powerful our witch Anthea had ever experienced. And the location was ideal. Remote in the mountains, with no way for the sort of overgrowth to happen as they'd seen in Massachusetts and New York. And Anthea had a plan to ensure it stayed that way, so the pack would never have to move on again.

She worked a spell that not only tapped into the earth magic, and her own ability to channel it—this time, she included the natural magic of the wolves by using the most powerful: the alpha's blood.

Blood magic was frowned upon, you understand. There were plenty of tales about rogue witches using blood to cast curses on former lovers or rivals. Blood magic was dark and dangerous. However, our alpha was willing to do whatever it took to find our pack a home, so she risked it all on the witch's word.

And it worked. The Smoky Falls Pack has lived here ever since. The magic is powerful, never fading, so long as a Harridan alpha leads the pack."

Mr. Carson sighs and takes another sip of his tea. Mine has gone cold in my cup; I've been too locked up in his story to think of the saucer on my lap.

"Now, we get into the more recent history. As Roxanne surely explained, the witches and seers became an even larger part of our pack dynamics. The alpha was required to take on as many mates as she could handle, in order to give every bloodline in the pack equal honor and responsibility of being alpha. There were four that felt their turns did not come as frequently, although out of eight original families, we were all quite intermingled at that point.

We had a family of witches who were also part of the pack. They came and went as they pleased, but always provided us a seer for the fated mates, and a witch whose sole responsibility was monitoring the pack's magical sanctuary.

When the pack split and the half went off to form their own pack, the pack seer and the pack witch were a pair of sisters, twins. The witch apparently felt her duties were less than her sister's, and resented that she didn't have the same level of glory among the pack. I'm not sure why, to be honest, as the witch was such a vital role. However, she resented it, and resented her sister.

Conspiring with what became Pack Montrose, she cast a spell on all of us to split the pack and sever the connection with the Harridan alpha, giving them the chance to have a new sanctuary, a new alpha. No one truthfully knows if the curse was intentional or not; they assume it was. But we only know that the result is that the Harridan alpha can't leave the sanctuary for over twenty-four hours at a time, and the entire pack can only shift between midnight and one."

I can't stop myself from interrupting. "But how did they figure that out? She had to have told *someone*. It seems pretty freaking specific."

Mr. Carson regards me with sadness in his gaze. "The alpha at that time went to the new pack's territory to try to reason with them. The split had torn her heart in half. She was suffering. Lilliana begged them to return, vowing to stay there until they agreed, and do whatever she had to in order to convince them to rejoin the pack. She died after twenty-four hours, and her younger sister became alpha at fifteen."

My throat is dry and tight; I swallow painfully and take a sip of my lukewarm tea. "That's one way to find out," I reply weakly.

"Indeed," he agrees. "That new alpha was your great grandmother. For tradition, she named her first daughter Lilliana, after her sister. She took on two more mates, and the cycle continued as if it had never been broken."

"Did she ever try to talk to the Montrose Pack?"

"Never. After the death of her sister, she shunned them completely."

"Has anyone tried to talk to them since?"

"No. The pack has a long memory, and the Montrose Pack watched your great aunt die, doing nothing to warn or save her."

"But, you just said they never knew if the witch who cast the curse meant for that to happen. Maybe it surprised them, too."

Mr. Carson's expression turns stony. "If they hadn't been greedy, and actually cared about what was best for the *pack*, none of it would have *ever* happened in the first place."

"I understand," I reply in my gentlest tone. "But it's possible that they regretted it, or that new generations regret it now. Maybe it would be worth reaching out to them-"

"No. Absolutely not." His reply is a harsh rebuke. "Your *duty* is to protect *your* pack, and those people decided long ago they no longer wanted that protection."

"But I don't want to be cursed for the rest of my life, either. What if there was a way to remove the curse, and people could shift again whenever they wanted? Wouldn't that be better for the pack?"

"Perhaps. Or you could die and take the sanctuary magic with you, leaving us all to slowly fade into depression and death." He stands abruptly, placing the delicate china cup and saucer back on the tray. "As the alpha, you can make the decisions you think are best for the pack; it is not my place to tell you either way. But as an old man speaking to a teenage girl who is new to this world, I would advise that you consider carefully the ramifications if you should fail."

Chapter Six

LAYLA

~

"... so that's the full story, I guess." I finish with a shrug, and swipe a French fry through the dregs of ketchup on my plate before popping it into my mouth.

The guys finished their food a while ago and have just listened, slack-jawed, while I go over what Mr. Carson told me.

"Wow," Milo finally says. "That's... that's a lot."

"We knew about the curse, but not how they figured it out," Jared agrees.

"Layla, how do you feel about it?" Landon's voice is soft.

"Helpless," I answer honestly. "I mean, this curse has been around that long and no one has tried to fix it?

They've just nursed this grudge for over a century and continued on with this miserable existence."

"I know it's not ideal, but it can't be that miserable," Milo says gently. "We're all still here and together. Your family has made sure of that."

"But my mom left to *escape* this place," I remind him. "She didn't want any part of this. She wanted out. She didn't want to be cursed."

"I can understand a teenage girl being afraid of such an enormous responsibility. I'm sure it was a lot to face on her own."

"She wasn't alone, any more than I am. She had her fated, and don't forget, she left two of them behind." The ache in my heart is real when I think about it. Just considering leaving one of these boys shoots a fresh bolt of panic through my chest. *Whoa, that's intense.* When did they go from being sexy friends I enjoyed having around to mates I'm terrified of losing?

The guys glance among themselves uneasily.

"Don't worry, I'm not going anywhere," I joke, trying to lighten the mood. "I'm already roped into the curse anyway, so you guys don't have to worry about it."

"Gee, thanks Layla, that's very comforting. Really makes a guy feel loved." Jared's tone is sarcastic enough that I know he's teasing even without the wink. Glancing at his watch, he sighs heavily. "Come on, Milo. We have to get to class. What are you punks going to do with your free afternoon?"

Since Landon and I have Thursday afternoon Bio

Lab, we don't have a class on Tuesdays. Now that I'm alpha, I've decided to take advantage of the opportunity to hang out in town, and told Maxwell to pick me up later. The weather is gorgeous, blue sky and sunshine with a comfortably crisp fall breeze. We skipped the cafeteria on campus and went into town for Badger's Burgers instead.

"I was thinking I'd show Layla around town some more, if that works for you?" He turns his soulful brown eyes on me, a wide grin sending flutters through my chest. Landon is always so sweet, so steadfastly supportive, that I sometimes forget how hot he is. But with his cleft chin, sharp jaw, and panty-dropping smile, I still hold my original impression that he looks like a rock star.

"Yeah, sounds like fun." I smile back, and then drop my gaze to my food to cool the heat in my cheeks.

Milo and Jared gather their trays, stopping to give me hugs before they leave. They've already promised to come to Harridan House for dinner, so I try not to be too sad they're leaving—I'll see them in just a few hours.

I know something is getting to them too. Jared's hug is tight and long, and he draws in a deep breath before he lets me go. But when Milo follows up, he turns and kisses my cheek before promising to see me later.

The first I find warm and comforting, if a little tingly. But the second sends heat racing through my chest at the memory of the kisses we shared.

They wave goodbye and walk out the door, and I

watch them go, evaluating my feelings curiously. While the kiss surprised me, the affection did not put me off in the least. It may have been weeks since we kissed, but I haven't stopped thinking about it, or stopped thinking about what it will be like to kiss all three of them. They say they're fine with the idea, have grown up knowing they'd share a mate and the position as alpha. But is it really that simple?

Milo's the only one I've even *kissed*… and I'm supposed to claim them as my mates when I take my position as alpha. It feels like so many huge decisions are rushing in on me with the speed and power of a freight train and I have no way of slowing them down.

It's not bad, although I don't feel like I'm in a relationship with them, it's definitely closer than just friends… is this because I like these guys, and they like me? Or is it just our fated mate's compulsion forcing us together?

I finish a few more fries before I give up, and Landon apparently reaches the bottom of his milkshake, the straw gurgling loudly at his attempts to get the last sip. When he catches me watching, his pursed lips curl into a smile. "Suppose it's time to admit defeat. You finished?" He gestures to my half-eaten food.

"Yeah, I'm done." We gather our trays and garbage and head outside together.

I've gone with yet another cropped sweater and a pair of faded jeans with wide legs and a high waist. Even though the sun is warm, the cool breeze worms its way under my shirt and chills my belly. I cross my arms over the exposed strip and glance up at Landon. "Okay, tour guide. Where are we going?"

He sets a large hand gently on my shoulder and turns me, pointing. "This way."

Without the other guys, he walks beside me now. I definitely feel tiny in comparison, nearly a foot shorter despite my thick-soled sneakers. Landon keeps his hand on my upper back as he guides me along the street, and even though it's unnecessary, it's nice. His warmth surrounds me like a reassuring blanket, and while every face we meet smiles in my direction, it's knowing that he has my back that truly makes me feel safe.

The scent of fall is on the air, even though the leaves have barely begun to turn. Something spicy and sweet drifts out of the open door of a home decor shop we pass; it's filled with ceramic pumpkins and kitschy signs. The sharp, earthy tang of the changing season blends with it, and I get a whiff of Landon's citrus scent like the icing on this deliciously perfect fall fragrance. If they sold it as a candle, I would definitely have Mrs. Dowling light them throughout the house. The thought makes me giggle, imagining how many candles it would take to fill Harridan House with one fragrance.

"Something funny?" Landon gazes down at me with a smile.

"I was just wondering if it would drive Mrs. Dowling crazy to have a ton of scented candles in Harridan House. You know, like a fall fragrance?" I draw in a deep breath. "I love fall."

"That surprises me; I would think, living in LA your whole life, that you never really got to experience it."

"Exactly! That's why it's my favorite."

Landon laughs. "You lost me."

"Well, my only experience with proper seasons was on TV. So I'd watch all the shows and see the seasons change. Of course, we had all the same stuff people have everywhere, fall candles and winter festivals with real pine wreaths, spring buttercups and tulips. I think my mom was so into the seasonal stuff because she missed it here." The sharp pang of sadness squeezes my chest; Mom loved filling our house with pumpkin spice candles. "She'd bake apple pies in the fall, and we'd have caramel popcorn and hot apple cider and watch Hocus Pocus." Even though I smile, the memory is tainted with sadness. When my parents died, those seasonal traditions were the thing I missed most.

"I loved that movie growing up," Landon admits, his warm hand rubbing my back in response to my sudden melancholy. "Did you watch The Grinch at Christmas, too?"

"Ha, of course! And we had hot cocoa with peppermint, and those Danish butter cookies that came in a tin."

"Oh my god, I love those things. I used to eat them by the fistful. You remember how they came in those paper wrappers, like four cookies each?" When I nod, he continues. "Milo, Jared and I would dare each other to eat more and more of them. One time we took the whole giant tin and made ourselves sick. Got a good

58

walloping once my mom realized what we'd done." He chuckles. "It was still worth it, though."

"That sounds like fun. I wish I had grown up with you guys. I bet we'd have lots of those kinds of memories."

Landon steers me gently into a right turn, and we keep following the sidewalk.

"We would, but it's okay that we don't, too," he replies gently. "We always knew you were out there, and we just couldn't wait to meet you. I think it's kind of fun that instead of growing up together, knowing each other's deep dark secrets, we get the chance to meet now. No missing teeth or skinned knees or kid fights. I think, given how our connection has always been here, that's kind of a special gift. Don't you?"

Landon's sudden seriousness takes me by surprise. There's a thread of deep emotion that stretches between him and me like a chord, tugging on my heart and drawing a surprising sting to my eyes.

"Perhaps," I agree, a little breathless. "But I've been alone for most of my life. I can't help wondering what it would have been like to have you guys there from day one, that's all."

"Well, I can tell you that if that were the case, I wouldn't have the distinct honor of bringing you here for the first time." Landon presses gently on my shoulder, turning me toward a storefront. It's small, with tall windows on either side of the door that are glazed and reflective.

But it's the sign above that forces me to catch my

breath: *The Olde Curiosity Shop - fancy used books and more.*

"Landon!" I gasp. "This is *awesome*. How did you know?"

"Eh," he blushes. "You always want to hang out in the library at Harridan House. Not that big of a leap."

"No, it's amazing, and I love it. Come on!" I grab his hand and tug toward the door, and his blush deepens. Somehow, he gets ahead and opens the door for me, leading me straight into Narnia.

Chapter Seven

LANDON

~

Being alone with Layla is quickly becoming my favorite form of torture.

I love my brothers; we've been bonded pretty much since birth. I have no qualms about sharing with them.

But having Layla to myself is even better than I imagined.

She loves the oddball little book store. Somehow, I just knew it was the right place to take her the second we got a chance. Dusty, stuffy air that stinks of old paper, and filled with rickety bookshelves overstuffed with ratty books—it's not exactly my scene.

However, none of that matters because I'm pretty sure Layla is in heaven. She keeps glancing at me with this huge smile, her brilliant green eyes glowing with excitement as she tugs my hand down another crooked row. My pulse pounds in my veins, the air around us taking on that electric quality that seems to happen whenever she's near.

Layla is chattering excitedly about some old book she found, dropping my hand to grab it and flip through the crumbling pages. I may grin like an idiot, but it's not for the same reason. I'm just pumped to have made her so happy. I could watch her all day, dogging her steps around the dusty stacks of recycled tree.

She's paused in front of a high window, golden beams of light shining all around her like a glowing aura she can't escape. I tuck my hands in my pockets to keep myself out of trouble, and lean against a nearby wall with a sigh. I dunno if she's gotten hotter in the last couple of months, or if the fated connection between us...

"Woah!" I nearly lose my balance as the shelf I was leaning against wobbles, sending a cascade of ancient books to the floor before I'm able to steady it and prevent the entire thing from tipping over. The noise is deafeningly loud in the near-silent book store.

Layla's eyes dart up to mine with shock, then she snort-laughs.

My cheeks are already flooded with heat and I glance down at the pile of books, dropping quickly to gather them up.

"What on *earth* is going on back there?" The creaky voice of the store owner carries around the dusty stacks. "I swear to the goddess, if you're making a mess, I'm going to call the pack beta…"

Layla snorts even louder and drops to her knees to help me. We quickly arrange the fallen books into a passably neat stack and shove it against the base of the shelf like several others. Her hands land on mine as we add the last few books, electric current passing between us at the touch, and our eyes meet.

"… Hooligans coming in here and making a mess," the shopkeeper's mutters are getting closer, along with a *thump-thump-thump* from her cane.

"Run for it!" I whisper, and Layla grins before popping up and tearing silently down the aisle, disappearing around a corner.

I'm hot on her heels, and I turn at the end of the row only to catch her whipping around the end of the next row, following the aisles like the curves of a snake.

In an open space I could catch her easily, but here my size is a disadvantage as I try to move quietly. I keep my shoulders drawn in to avoid bumping any more bookshelves, and I can't get up to full speed before I hit another corner.

The heat of embarrassment has left my face, but now it's just a game of 'keep away from the ornery shop keeper' who clearly didn't realize exactly *who* is in her store right now. If she did, she certainly wouldn't be threatening to call Roxanne on us like a couple of misbehaving teenage punks. I can hear her shouting something in the distance, but it's muffled behind so many twisted shelves of books.

When I turn another corner, I run smack into Layla who is already braced and waiting to catch me. She stops me with both hands to my stomach, which tightens instinctively, before she lifts one finger to her lips with a conspiratorial glint in her eyes.

My chest is heaving for air, and all I can think about is the warmth of her hand through my shirt and how those lips would feel pressed against mine—*super* jealous of that finger. I try to pay attention to whatever she's listening for, and then I hear it: faint music as the radio at the front desk clicks on, ostensibly because the owner has returned to her stool and is no longer trying to follow us.

Grinning wickedly, Layla returns the hand to my chest and pushes me backward into a low shelf of books that—mercifully—rests against a wall so it doesn't topple over. It bites into the backs of my legs and I wince, almost complaining, before I see the look in her eyes.

There's only one description for the way she's looking at me right now, and it makes every muscle in my body tighten as my pulse starts racing: Layla's gaze is *hungry*.

Layla

I don't know what's gotten into me, but after tearing through the bookshelves like naughty kids evading a punishment, there's only one thought on my mind when Landon whips around the corner.

The intense, burning need to kiss him.

We're both panting lightly from our silent game of racing through the stacks, and when I reach up and tug his face down to mine, his breath is warm on my cheek. The electric sensation I've come to associate with my fated skitters across my skin, radiating from where our bodies touch outward and filling me with a growing sense of excitement. Instinctively, I rise to my toes to meet him, and my fingers thread through the short, silky hair at the back of his neck.

There's a brief, tingling moment where his soulful eyes lock on mine, and it's as if we're waiting to find out who will make the first move. I can scarcely breathe; the air is so thick with anticipation it's like my lungs are unable to draw it in.

Then, as if we've silently agreed, we both move forward as one.

Landon's lips are soft and warm, and a light jolt of electricity passing between us the second we connect draws out the moment in a deliciously torturous way. He freezes on instinct, but as soon as I tighten my fingers on his neck, he kisses me in earnest.

At first it's just gentle presses of his mouth against

mine, and it's warm and sweet and I breathe him in, enjoying the moment. The two of us, alone, kissing among the hidden stacks of books that rarely see a visitor.

But instinct soon takes over. Landon's hands have hung limply by his side, but now they rise, long fingers splaying around my hips and drawing me against his body, igniting more of those delicious tingles. His head tilts, and he presses more firmly against me, seeking entrance to my mouth with his tongue while my arms wrap around his neck, drawing him even closer. My lips part to let him in, and the electric sensation heightens.

My heart is pounding now. I feel it battering against the cage of my chest while our kisses become even more frenzied.

As if he's tired of bending down, Landon's large hands grip my butt and lift me, pulling me tightly to his body as he swings around to set me on the low shelf he was leaning against seconds before. My legs wrap around his lean frame and hook together, squeezing him even tighter.

Now I'm closer to his height and the angle is much better for kissing. With his arms braced on the wall to either side, I press my chest to his, relishing the flood of sensations coursing over my skin. Even though we're both wearing sweaters, the heat of his body leeches into mine, along with faint tingles that the fabric fails to stop. My hands clench in his baby-soft hair, tightening and tugging lightly. A low rumble sounds in Landon's chest; it resonates through mine, and my heart rate climbs even higher in response. There's something so wild, so *animal* about it, that my body responds viscerally, my movements growing more frantic. It's a raw, feral side of Landon I've never seen. I'm starving for air, but at this moment I couldn't pull my lips from his if I wanted to.

And I certainly don't want to.

However, Landon chooses this moment to rip his mouth from mine, leaving me panting while he trails kisses along my jaw to my neck. His breath is hot and ragged, and every new contact sends a fresh course of trembles through my body. Heat ripples across my skin, building in my core and making me shift uncomfortably on my perch. My legs tighten and draw him even closer, the pressure where our bodies meet hot and irresistible. I can't stop from rubbing myself against him.

The low growl in Landon's throat grows louder, and he nips at my earlobe. "Layla," he purrs in a deep, rough voice. "While this is super hot, I'm not sure I can focus a hundred percent while listening for approaching footsteps."

He follows up that very practical sentiment by drawing my earlobe between his soft lips, then dragging it between his teeth, which nearly turns me into a puddle on the spot.

As if knowing I can't help myself, Landon pulls in a deep, shuddering breath, then squeezes me against his chest. It forces me to draw in my own ragged gasps and try to shove the lustful animal that had come roaring out of me back into her cage. I wrap my arms around his waist and try to steady my breathing, Landon's warm breath stirring my hair as he rests his chin on my head.

After a few moments we've calmed somewhat, although my pants are uncomfortably hot and my need for satisfaction has not abated. However, I *have* regained control of my body; at least enough that I'm not likely to pounce on him like a spider monkey and force my tongue down his throat.

I lean back and catch Landon's gaze. His face is flushed, cheeks adorably pink with high spots of color, and his rich, soulful eyes swim with emotion as he gazes back at me.

"Hi," he says awkwardly.

"Hi," my response is equally shy in the wake of our sudden frenzy.

Deciding he needs me to take the lead, I reach up with both hands and grasp his face lightly, pulling him in for one more soft, chaste kiss. Then I smile. "Come on, let's get out of here."

Landon's answering smile is brilliant, and I melt again, just a little. He helps me down from the shelf and when I intertwine my fingers with his, his grin widens. We take our time weaving our way out of the bookstore, stopping only to pick up the tattered hard cover of Sense & Sensibility that I'd dropped in our mad escape from the shopkeeper. I do my best to act completely innocent as we approach the front counter, but I'm sure we aren't the first people to knock something over and make out in the back. Her suspicious gaze tells me as much while she scans the sticker. After I pay for the book—Landon tries to buy it for me, but I insist—we make our way back outside into the bright fall sunshine.

Tingles continue to course through my body, and I refuse to drop Landon's hand.

Chapter Eight

LAYLA

~

After the rush of making out, it takes a while for the sexual tension thrumming in my veins to quiet down. Landon keeps his promise of showing me around town, and we stop into a few stores he frequents, as well as a few he clearly thinks I would like. He does well with the bookshop, followed by one selling fudge and other handmade treats, a new coffee place I've never been to, and an obvious tourist trap filled with kitschy, bear-themed merchandise that makes me giggle. But when he tugs me around a corner to a new storefront, I pull up short.

"Clothes?" I glance up at him in surprise, tugging on his arm. He hasn't dropped my hand since we left the bookstore, and I've been enjoying the warm tingles.

Apparently, my face shows my opinion on the matter, because his hopeful expression drops.

"Uh, yeah? I mean, I thought girls liked clothes?" He scratches the back of his neck awkwardly and diverts his eyes to the window display, filled with fashionable outfits. "You always dress so cute, I just assumed you'd like it..." the spots of color are back on his cheeks, and it makes me my heart flip-flop in my chest.

I haven't forgotten my first impression of him looking like a broody rock star with those soulful eyes and pouty lips. But knowing how sweet and awkward he actually is feels even better, like a secret between us two.

"I wish I could claim credit for my 'style', but I have to lay that firmly on Roxanne," I confess. "I haven't picked out a stitch of clothing in my wardrobe. Swear to god. I have the worst fashion sense. But it means a lot that you think I always look cute." I wrap my free hand around the back of his, and tug him down to my level so I can kiss his cheek. "For future reference, clothes really aren't my jam. I'd probably wear the same thing every day if I didn't have a fashionable beta stocking my closet. You have more fashion sense than I do," I gesture at his outfit. "You always look nice, too."

The color in his cheeks deepens. "Honestly, Milo picks out most of my clothes. He kind of tosses things at me and tells me to buy them. I don't even know my own size anymore."

A laugh barks from my lips. "Now *that* I do believe. At least he doesn't dress you like himself. At any rate, he seems to have a handle on your style. It looks good on you."

"I'll let him know you think so," Landon grins.

"Do that. Does he pick out Jared's clothes, too?" Now I'm curious about the guys' dynamic. What other quirks do I not know yet?

"Ha, mister 'brand t-shirt and jeans every day?' Definitely not. He tried and failed to give Jared a makeover when we were in high school. Jared stopped him straight up." He leans in conspiratorially. "I think Jared's mom still picks out his clothes, to be honest. I don't think Jared cares all that much. He just didn't want Milo to have his way."

I snort in amusement—I can see that. "I know you guys all consider yourselves brothers, but they seem to have a more... sibling-like relationship than you do with either of them, if I'm honest." I tug his hand and we turn, walking back toward the main street.

"If you mean they tease each other a lot, yeah, I'd agree. They like to bicker more than I do. But I wouldn't say they're closer than I feel to either of them... it's just our dynamic."

"Jared is the goofy jock, Milo is the opinionated, coffee-drinking hipster, and you're the sweet one." I smile up at him, but don't miss the grimace that crosses his face in the wake of my statement. "Oh no, is that bad? I like that you're sweet!"

He shrugs, dropping his eyes to the ground. "I dunno. I guess it makes me sound kind of boring. My only personality trait is being sweet?"

Embarrassment floods my chest. "I'm sorry, that's not what I meant at all. You're always so thoughtful of everyone around you. I feel you don't talk about yourself as much. Maybe I should grill you for more details. Tell me more about Landon."

The color returns to his cheeks. "I dunno what to say. I don't think I'm very interesting."

"I hardly believe that. Do you have a secret passion? A hidden talent? Do you like to knit scarves in your spare time?" I nudge him with my shoulder and squeeze his hand.

It has the desired effect, and Landon grins. "No, I don't knit. Thank god, that would be embarrassing. Um, I play the guitar? But that's not very interesting. Tons of people do it."

"I think it's interesting, and I don't know anyone else who does. Like what kind of guitar? What do you like to play?"

"Mostly acoustic. I started with ballads, like John Mayer, Jack Johnson kind of stuff. Now I mainly play my own songs."

I stop dead in my tracks. "Landon, you *write* music? That's so *cool*. Why didn't you say something? Will you play one for me?"

His gaze returns to his feet. "It's not as cool as it sounds, I swear. I dunno. I don't talk about it much because it's just fooling around. And then people want to hear me play and it's embarrassing, I don't play in front of people."

"Oh, so you don't like to have people watch you.

Well, that I can understand. Have Jared or Milo seen you play?"

"Yeah, but just other people's songs. I've never played them any of my own. They're too personal."

The anxiety rolling off of him at the idea of playing for other people is palpable. My heart clenches; this was clearly difficult for him to share.

"Well, I would love to hear you, but only if you want me to." I give his hand another squeeze and tug gently to get us moving again. "You know, when I first saw you in the greenhouse, my first impression was that you looked like a rock star."

Peeking up at him, I catch his blush deepen. "You didn't really think that."

"No, seriously, I did! You have the look. I even remember thinking to myself that even if you were terrible, I'd still go see you play because you were that hot."

That statement draws a chuckle from him. "Well, that's reassuring."

"That was meant to be a compliment, you know. I'm not trying to say I assume you're bad. In fact, I bet you're amazing."

"Don't get your expectations too high, or I'll never live up to them. Besides, you can't just look at a person and know they're good at something."

"I disagree. You've got long, delicate fingers, so I bet you do really well at reaching the chords. And you have a really rich, smooth voice, so I can imagine what you'd sound like singing. I bet you're great."

Landon looks distinctly uncomfortable in the wake of all my praise. "I think you're being way too generous. I just mess around with it."

"Well, I guess I won't know for sure until I hear you play." I shrug. "Until then, I'll just keep assuming what I want."

"I suppose that's fair."

He tugs me around another corner, and we pass back into light, playful banter for the rest of the afternoon.

A few hours later I'm in my room alone for once, trying to focus on homework, when my phone pings.

I take a few minutes before I check the message, but as soon as I do, my pulse quickens.

It's from Landon, and it's an audio file.

Excitement tingling over my skin, I sprawl out on my bed and hit play.

"Hey Layla." Landon's voice is shaky, his nerves coming across the recording viscerally, and my heart thumps painfully for him. "I've never done this before, but you wanted to hear me play, and I don't want you to think my defining characteristic is 'sweet', so I figured this was a good place to start."

Anticipation is thrumming through my body now, and I wait eagerly through some rustling noises and the faint sound of the guitar strings being brushed.

Lightly at first, then with growing confidence, a

melody starts, followed by chords that add depth to the music. And just as I expected, it's perfect. Beautifully played, not a single mistake I can hear. A sweet, rich, and slightly wistful song that resonates through the wooden body of the guitar and fills my ears.

And then Landon starts singing.

Just as with the playing, it starts off softly, so low I can barely hear him over the guitar itself. But he grows in confidence and the notes become richer, inflected with more emotion.

Goosebumps rise across my skin—he's *fantastic*. His voice is so beautiful it brings tears to my eyes. It's a simple song, talking about a day spent with his friends, and I can tell he's completely lost in it right up until the end.

The sound of his hand pressing on the strings to stop the guitar reverberations jolts me out of the musical spell, and Landon coughs awkwardly. "Well, there you have it. A Landon Crews original, for an audience of one. I hope it lived up to your expectations. Goodnight, Layla."

My heart races in my chest, and I rush to record a voice note of my own, fully aware that he's probably sweating bullets waiting for my reply.

"Landon, that was *amazing*. You are even better than I expected, I really mean it. Thanks so much for sharing that with me. It… means a lot, that you played for me. Seriously, I love it. Thank you." I send it off and after a few moments he replies with a kissy-face emoji and the words, "For you Layla, anything."

Making out with him this afternoon was hot, but somehow this is even hotter.

The way the guys all share everything, and our status as fated mates, I sort of felt like I would just be another thing they shared.

Now that we could all have something special, something only each guy and I share, is an exciting prospect. I resolve to spend more time with each of them alone, so I can really try to develop the relationship we're apparently fated to have.

Beyond the initial attraction and—I'm assuming—fated connection I feel toward all of them, I need more. Lust is great and exciting, but I know myself, and I don't open up easily to other people. People I counted on have burned me too many times. It's almost painful to expose myself to that kind of anguish again. I shy away from even the idea of counting on others in any significant way.

But how can I claim these guys as my fated, curse them to the same fate I've been tricked into, if I don't forge genuine connections with them? Connections that go beyond lust or attraction, connections that are deep and earth-shattering and *true*?

My mind, bizarrely, flips to Derrek out of nowhere. When we lived on the streets, I trusted him implicitly. I believed with my whole heart that he would always protect me, always look out for me, be there if I needed him. In the year I spent after the attack, my belief was shattered repeatedly, waiting for him to turn up.

Now, of course, I know what happened, and that he

didn't just abandon me. I have the full story, but I don't feel like it's taken away the hurt I still feel. Some part of me needs more.

Resolving to speak to him after class, I hit 'play' on Landon's recording, and listen to him on repeat with my eyes closed, just picturing what he would look like, singing for an audience of one.

Chapter Nine

JARED

~

"I don't like the guy." I can't keep the growl out of my voice, thinking about this dude from Layla's past who just shows up and acts like he owns a piece of her. My eyes remain glued to the road as I pull in to the Painted Moose drive-thru.

"I don't disagree with you," Milo comments from the passenger seat, "but I doubt acting territorial around Lex is going to help our cause any."

"Well, she's *our* fated. I think it's only natural to feel a little territorial, given that we finally just got her and this smoothie-smarty-pants professor type—if he even really *is* a professor—swoops in after leaving Layla out in the cold for a year."

Milo snorts. "Yes, he really is a professor, and he didn't exactly leave Layla out in the cold. You're being dramatic. She was with Roxanne that whole time. From what she says, he took care of her—and a lot of other kids—sort of like an older brother."

"Yeah well, she's not looking at him like he's an older brother," I grumble, then lean toward the window to place our order.

"I think you need to stop worrying about what you *think* and instead focus on what you know," he replies in a gentler tone. "She's our fated, she knows it, she's here on pack territory, and he's just some guy that's distantly related to the pack seer."

"I dunno, until she accepts us as her fated, I *know* I'm going to be on edge about it. You know what happened with her mom, how it affected Amber's dad. My auntie said he was a really nice dude until Lilliana Harridan split. That being rejected twisted him up inside." I pull ahead and join the line for pick up.

"Well, don't forget that Lex's mom skipped town before she manifested. Lex can't do that. She's already become the alpha. I'd say the chances of her rejecting us are slim." Milo is infuriatingly calm and self-assured.

"You heard her, questioning why we would want to be cursed just like her? She's not sold." After accepting the three drinks—one for Layla, obviously—I pull back out onto the main road, heading for campus. "Unless something changes dramatically, I'm going to be on edge until the eclipse."

Milo sighs, pulling the lid from his cup and dumping in sugar. "Well, I don't know what to tell you. I don't have a remedy for your fears, other than to tell you to spend more time with her doing something *other* than reciting your cheesy jokes."

"I'm not sure you realize this, but my schedule is more complicated than yours and Landon's." I sound defensive, but I can't help it. "I barely get out of practice with enough time to eat dinner and do my homework. I thought college was supposed to be more *fun* than high school, not just more work."

"That's what you get for being Mr. All-American captain of the football team." Milo smirks at me from behind his dark glasses. "This is why I prefer not to take part in team activities in general."

"You're hilarious. But seriously, help me get some time with Layla, figure out something we can do together. Sundays are the best bet, since I won't have a game or practice. And last year I was captain, this year I'm just a freshman tight end."

"I'll think about it," he concedes. "In the meantime, try not to be obvious around her how you feel about the new prof. You'll just upset her."

"Fine, fine," I grumble. "I'll be cool as a cucumber."

∽

Layla

I didn't have time to speak with Derrek before class, so I sit through the entire lecture, twitching with nerves. I'm not sure exactly what I'm going to say, but it'll be something along the lines of really telling him how hurt I was not to see him and all the rest of my friends in the aftermath of my attack. I know it won't change the past, and that a big part of it was Dom and Roxanne's interference, which neither of us are responsible for.

Still, I feel a deep, driving need to finally pour this feeling out into the open, set it free so I can stop harboring it deep in my chest. Something is telling me that saying it out loud, really letting him know how disappointed I felt, is going to help me.

And I need to see his reaction, gauge his response to me confessing those feelings.

Because I'm so tied up in my own brain, I take nearly to the end of class to realize that Jared has been quiet and tense beside me for the whole class. Typically he's slipping me a note, or making some kind of commentary under his breath throughout the hour.

When I glance at him, curious about this change in behavior, I'm surprised to find he's glaring at Derrek with barely contained fury. His brows are low over his dark eyes, with one fist clenched on his leg. The other hand has a pencil twirling madly through the air, end over end, while his knee jostles.

I tone down my emotions and realize I'd tuned him out completely. *Huh, well, it's good to know I've figured out how to do that.*

Now that I'm looking for them, Jared's emotions hit me like a sledgehammer. He's angry and suspicious. Furious, to the point he might as well be screaming it.

"Hey," I whisper, leaning in his direction. "You okay?"

He seems to startle out of his trance, and settles back, releasing his fist before grinning back at me. "Yeah, what's up?"

"You just seem upset," I hint, not adding that it was a bit more than 'seem' based on my alpha senses.

"Just got a lot on my mind, with class and football and stuff," he shrugs. "Nothing for you to worry about."

I raise one eyebrow. *Really?* He should know better than trying to BS me like that.

Jared's dark eyes dart to the front of the lecture hall. "Okay, fine," he sighs quietly. "I don't like the new prof. I don't like that he lied to you about who he was, that he turned up here out of the blue, and I especially don't like that he hurt you."

My heart thumps, warmth spreading through my chest. "Thanks, but you don't have to worry about me. I'm working on it. Alpha, remember?" I tease quietly, pointing to myself.

Jared's eyes darken, and he leans closer to me, grasping my hand with warm, strong fingers. "Well, you should remember that as your fated, your pain is my pain. Your happiness is my happiness. And once you claim us, that makes us alphas, too. It's impossible for me to separate my needs from yours. I need for you

87

to be happy, and I don't trust *him* because he broke *your* trust."

I stare at Jared as if I've never seen him before. This heartfelt speech seems so unlike him; not the goofy jokester I've become accustomed to. There's real feeling behind this, and I know I need to tread carefully.

"Thank you," I whisper back. "It means more than I can say that you care so deeply about my feelings. But please respect that I want to handle this in my own way?"

Jared holds my gaze for a long second, then nods, releasing my hand and leaning back in his seat to stare forward once more.

When class finally finishes, he stands and waits for me to pack up my things.

"You go on ahead," I tell him. "I'm going to have a word with the professor."

His jaw clenches, the muscle working a few times in rapid succession as he stares at me, then he nods. "Okay, I'll talk to you later, Layla."

Hurt rolls off of him in palpable waves, but I can only deal with one person's emotions right now, and for the time being, that person is me.

"Lex, great to see you again!" Derrek beams when I reach the bottom of the stairs. "What did you think of the lesson? I know you've always been an avid reader, so I was excited to have you in this class. Are you looking forward to our open discussion on Friday?"

"Um, yeah," I mutter, embarrassed. I didn't pay

attention to a word he said today. Hopefully, I didn't miss anything too important.

"I actually wanted to talk to you about something else."

Derrek settles back on the desk. Today he's wearing dark jeans with another dress shirt and tie, his sandy blonde curls disheveled as if he's been running his fingers through them. I suddenly remember him running a hand over his shaved head a lot when we were on the street. "Sure, go ahead."

My mouth is a desert. I glance around, waiting for the last straggling student to leave the classroom before I clear my throat to speak. "Um, I know we kind of talked about it on Monday, but there's something else I need to tell you. About LA."

Discomfort darkens his green eyes, and he shifts slightly. "Okay, I'm listening."

I wipe sweaty palms on my jeans; my heart is racing, and I'm trying to remember why I thought it was a good idea to confess these feelings I've kept locked away for so long. My eyes drop to the ground as I gather my courage.

"Um, well, I was really upset that I never saw you again after the attack."

"I know, Lex, I'm sorry. Like I said, I-"

"No, let me finish. I know you didn't realize I was there. And I don't blame you for it, but I was *really* hurt, even more than I realized." My heart beats like a frightened bird trying to escape a cage, but I draw in a deep breath and lift my head, gazing straight into his sympathetic green eyes. "I trusted you, more than I knew at the time. I trusted you like *family*, and then I just... never saw you again. After my parents, I thought I was alone in the world, and losing you felt like that happened all over again. Sure, my uncle appeared out of nowhere, and now we're here and I have all of this," I gesture around, trying to wordlessly indicate Smoky Falls and everyone in it.

"But I never got over it, and I sort of feel like something in me broke; feeling like I lost you, the one person I thought I could trust after I lost *everything* I'd ever had. And you can't imagine the guilt I felt, wanting to go back and see everyone and not being able to convince my feet to move. Now I understand it was compulsion and I can almost forgive myself for it. I didn't know what was happening and I couldn't help it.

"But I can't forgive you for showing up here and acting like none of that ever happened. You had a way to get ahold of me, a contact. You could have tried harder, and knowing that you didn't so much as *try* hurts more than any of it." The last part comes out in a whisper, and I draw in a shaky breath to hold back the threatening sobs; I promised myself I wouldn't cry. "So I guess that's it," I sniff. "I needed to say it, to get it out of me and hope it helps me to let it go. I don't expect you to do anything about it, not that there's anything you can do. But I wanted you to know."

Derrek has frozen completely with his gaze locked on my face, and I question if he's even breathing.

Then, in one swift move, he pushes off the desk and

wraps me into a hug, pulling me into his hard body and squeezing tightly. Warmth spreads through me, heat from his body near mine, but also emotion welling inside my chest. I bite my lip to keep the tears at bay. I draw in another shaky breath, his smoky bourbon scent filling my senses, and I notice something else: a faint electric tingle coursing over my skin.

"Lex," he breathes into my hair, pressing a kiss to the top of my head. "I'm so sorry. I thought you were *safe*, that you were finally loved and happy and didn't need me anymore. If I'd have thought for a *second* that you needed me, nothing would have stopped me from reaching you."

The emotion I was desperately holding back overflows the banks of my heart and I sob heavily, squeezing my face against his chest. *This* is what I needed, what I came looking for without realizing it. To know that I mattered just as much to him as he had mattered, *still* matters, to me.

Derrek's arms tighten around me, and he presses a cheek to the crown of my head. "I'm here, and I'm not going anywhere, Lex. If you need me, if you want me, I'll *never* leave."

The relief that flows through my heart at those words is indescribable. I draw in a deep, shuddering breath, then sigh, releasing the pain that has dragged me down for over a year. The nebulous implication of those words tingles at the edge of my mind, wondering if he means them with any more significance than just as a friend.

I wonder if I *want* them to mean more.

Then an angry voice interrupts the moment and sends us jumping apart. My senses reach out instinctively, picking up three bright balls of emotion just steps away.

"Get your paws off our *mate*."

Chapter Ten

LAYLA

~

"Guys, what are you doing here?" Even though I'm technically doing nothing wrong, my voice sounds distinctly guilty. Some part of me knows that, innocent or not, this looks bad and they have a valid reason to be upset.

My gaze travels between three very different expressions, my eyes darting back and forth nervously in the heavy silence.

Jared's face is pure fury—I know he was already suspicious about my relationship with Derrek, and this probably added fuel to the fire.

Milo wears a darkly amused expression, keeping the truth of his emotions concealed better, at least visibly. Thanks to my alpha senses, I can tell he's not nearly as calm as he pretends to be.

Landon simply looks surprised and hurt, which matches his emotional landscape.

"Jared was worried about you," Milo finally answers in a slow drawl, as if he doesn't really care. "So he asked us to meet him here. He was concerned the new Lit professor would try to make a move on you. Seems he was right to be concerned."

Derrek bristles at my side, but I step in front of him and hold up a hand. Indignation burns in my veins at the implication, and I need to stop this mess before it becomes a disaster. "First of all, he didn't 'make a move on me'. We had some things to hash out from the past, and we shared a hug. End of story.

"Second, I am the alpha, and while you might be my fated mates, I have yet to accept you. We may have a connection, but for the most part, I barely know you. I've known Derrek for *years*. He's like a long-lost member of my family, and you all have no place to interfere. So I suggest you dial it back a bit and stop presuming to own me."

Milo's eyes widen and his expression goes slack with the surprise I feel across our bond. Landon looks distinctly guilty, and his emotions color to match.

But Jared's expression and feelings don't change. He remains angry, and instead of saying anything, he turns and marches out of the door.

Derrek places a warm palm on my shoulder, and I draw comfort from it. Light tingles course over my skin at the contact once again, and I step out of his reach before I can think too much about what it means.

Instead, I turn and give him a smile, murmuring, "I'll see you Friday," and then join the two fated who wait for me by the doorway.

We walk in silence down the empty hallway for a few moments before Milo says, "Well, that was interesting."

I snort, grateful for the return of his playful tone and somewhat pleased with how I stood up for myself. "Yeah, I'll say."

"Layla," Landon's voice is soft. "You know we don't think we own you, right? We care about you, and being fated comes with a connection that sometimes triggers a very... possessive response, but we respect you completely."

A dry chuckle escapes my lips. "Yeah, maybe you should tell Jared that. What is with him, anyway? He was mad throughout class. I tried to explain to him but I guess it didn't take."

"Jared doesn't see you as a possession either, I promise. He's just always been very protective. Even toward us."

"It's true, Lex. When we were younger, this one," Milo shoves Landon playfully in the shoulder, "was a real runt. Some of the bigger boys picked on him and Jared made sure they regretted it." He drapes an arm around my shoulder and leans in with that sexy smirk. "I'd love to see you take Jared down a peg. He's been the football golden boy for quite some time now. I think it'd be hilarious to see him squirm under your alpha command. And sexy."

Heat slithers over my skin at the way he says 'sexy'. "I wouldn't use that on you guys, though. Not after finding out Roxanne used it on me for over a year. It feels… like a dirty trick to pull, taking away someone's free will."

"Nah," Landon grabs my hand, threading his fingers through mine. "We're all used to it. It's just part of pack life. Otherwise, people would be constantly fighting over stupid stuff. We don't randomly wolf out anymore like they used to, but people still get stupid upset for dumb shit."

"Wolf out?"

"Yeah. I guess—back before there was a curse, people would shift on the drop of a hat. A lot of times, anger was the trigger. I suppose that might still happen in other packs, but here, we can't shift even if we want to, unless it's between midnight and one."

"Huh. I guess I've never known anything else, so I didn't think about it."

Landon shrugs. "Yeah, me neither. But I guess when you get really angry and feel that crawling sensation under your skin, that's your wolf trying to get out."

"How do you know that?"

"My dad told me."

Milo snorts. "Sounds like another Crews Classic to me."

"No, it's true!"

My eyes dart to Milo. "Crews Classic?"

"Yeah. Landon's dad is known for making up shit to scare us or just trick us. He's done it since we were kids."

"Why?"

"Just being a dad, I suppose. He got a kick out of telling us the garbage can actually eats the garbage, stuff like that. As we got older, he tried to make it scarier, usually stuff to keep us in line. If we didn't take the garbage out at night, the can would come into the house, hunting us."

"That seems… odd. But fun!" I correct quickly, not wanting to hurt Landon's feelings. "It sounds like he has a good sense of humor."

"I know which of his stories are real and which are made up," Landon mutters. "I'm not a complete idiot."

"Of course you're not," I reassure him.

"If you say so," Milo shrugs as we pass through the glass doors into brilliant sunshine. "So, what should we do with this beautiful fall afternoon?"

A sigh escapes my lips. "I have to head back to Harridan House. Roxanne texted me I have some alpha stuff to do."

"No problem," Landon grins. "Let's get our alpha home so she can get to work."

"I'm sorry, *what* is the issue?"

We're in Roxanne's modest Toyota, driving back into town, and she's explaining what we're about to face.

"Mrs. Angleton has a Pomeranian. Her neighbor, Mr. Fredricks, claims that the dog poops in his yard every day, and she doesn't pick it up. She insists the dog only poops in *her* yard, and he's just harassing her.

"This is not the first time he's complained about it. I've suggested he get a camera so he can get proof, but he's an older gentleman and doesn't want to deal with technology. He insists the poop is proof enough."

The laughter ripples from my chest. "This is the big serious alpha duty my uncle dealt with? Good lord. Now I understand where the alpha command comes in. Why can't they just sort it out?"

Roxanne's voice is patient, but firm. "As the alpha, it's your job to sort out disputes, no matter how silly they may seem to you, with as little forced compliance as possible. This issue is a serious problem for them. Thus, it's a serious problem for you. In a normal society, they'd report it to the police, but here..."

"Here, the job falls to me," I sigh. "I get it. So what do I do?"

"Well, I want you to listen to their complaints and see where your instincts lead you. Your inner alpha should help you find a way through, so I don't want to lead the witness." She slows the car, pulling into the driveway of a small but neat little gingerbread house of a home. An older woman stands on the tiny porch in a pink housecoat, clutching a tan fluffy dog with a pink bow between its ears.

We barely open the doors of the car before she

comes shuffling over in her slippers, jabbering. Obviously agitated, words fly out of her a mile a minute.

"Thank you so much for coming, alpha. I just don't know what to do with that bully. I told him Princess never leaves the house without me, and she only does her business in my backyard, and I pay the neighbor boy twenty dollars a week to clean it up. There's no way the poop in his yard is hers, but he keeps blaming it on poor Princess, shouting over the fence at us and scaring her half to death." The old woman strokes a trembling, age-spotted hand over the dog's head. The animal seems completely at ease, her panting snout practically smiling.

The dog is *really* cute. I'm already biased.

Trying not to be distracted, I word my response carefully based on the lesson I had with Roxanne. "Thank you for bringing this to my attention. What resolution are you hoping to reach?"

She looks at me as if I'm stupid. "Well, for that old bully to stop shouting at me and blaming Princess for the poop, obviously."

I swallow down the sudden urge to giggle. "Okay, let me speak with Mr. Fredricks and see what he has to say."

"I know what he'll say. He'll say the same thing he's been saying for months. But he's wrong!" She wags a gnarled finger at me.

"Okay, Mrs. Angleton, I'll be right back." I turn and walk the few steps toward the neighbor's house. Naturally, he's been watching us through the screen door the entire time and is out on the porch, shouting, before I reach him.

"I've been saying it for months, and it keeps happening. That rat needs to stop pooping on my lawn!"

"She's a dog, and she's not pooping on your lawn, you senile old codger," Mrs. Angleton shouts back from her driveway. "Princess is a good girl and always goes poopy where she's supposed to."

"Bah," he shouts back. "No one in their right mind would call that thing a dog. At best, she's a rabbit." He turns to glare at me, brown hands on his hips. His pants are pulled up over his belly button, held in place by a pair of brightly colored suspenders, worn over a simple white tank top despite the chilly fall air. "Come here, alpha, I'll show you all the proof you need. She did it again, and I left it so you can see." He waves a hand, the long skin of his upper arm dangling with the gesture, and I follow his short steps along the side of his house to a small patch of grass just past his driveway. A tall wooden fence separates his property from Mrs. Angleton's, shaded by a robust maple tree whose leaves are turning a brilliant shade of orange.

Sure enough, there's a tiny, dark pile of poop right in the middle of an otherwise emerald green lawn.

"You see?" He crows triumphantly. "Proof that rat shit on my lawn."

It is *killing* me, but somehow I maintain a straight face. Roxanne wasn't kidding; they take this very seriously despite how silly it seems to me, and I have to be respectful.

I look closely at the offending pile and quickly conclude that this is not Pomeranian poo. But the trick is convincing him of that fact.

"Thank you, Mr. Fredricks. Would you excuse me for just a minute? I need to speak with your neighbor." I turn and head back to his driveway, where Roxanne and Mrs. Angleton are waiting, pom in hand.

"HA!" He shouts. "You see, you crazy old bat? I told you the alpha would take care of it. Now you're in trouble."

Ignoring him, I head straight for the older woman. "Ma'am, when was the last time the neighbor cleaned up your backyard for you?"

"He comes every Saturday, so it's been a few days. Why?"

"Would you be ok if we brought your neighbor to your yard so he could see that the poop in his yard is not the same?"

"Well, certainly, if it would get him to SHUT UP!" Her voice goes from sweet to surly in a second as she shouts the last two words at him. "This way, through the gate."

"Mr. Fredricks, why don't you come with us for a minute?"

"Bah, no thank you. I don't want to see a giant pile of poop. I've got enough to deal with in my own yard."

"Well, this is your opportunity to prove you're right," I coax. "Don't you want to be vindicated?"

"Well, I mean, I should think the poop itself is proof enough," he grumbles. "But fine, I'll go."

Hitching up his pants—I'm amazed they can go any higher—he starts a slow march around the fence to the neighboring driveway and up, and Roxanne and I follow like a slow, bizarre parade.

We finally make it into the backyard, which is nearly filled with flower gardens, birdbaths, and an insane amount of garden decor like ceramic toadstools and fairy balls. The one little strip of grass that weaves neatly through the encroaching gardens is bright green, and littered with tiny tan turds.

"You see, you old coot? Princess could hardly be pooping in your yard when she's clearly doing her business here." The elderly woman spits at her neighbor.

"That doesn't mean anything," he fires back. "Dogs can shit more than once a day. Besides, she's out here all the time, barking her head off. I can never relax on my own damn back porch."

"Mr. Fredricks, do you notice anything about this poop compared to the one on your lawn?"

"Yeah, there's a lot more of it," he snorts. "Which I suppose is good."

"No, I mean the fact that it's smaller and a completely different color than the poop on your lawn."

"So? She ate some blueberries or sommat and took a bigger poop. On purpose!" He fires at the older woman.

I lay a gentle hand on his arm. "Mr. Fredricks, I believe it was a natural assumption that the dog next door was leaving poop in your yard, but have you actually ever seen her do it?"

"Well, no, it's always in the dead of night. I don't go out for the shift as often as I used to, but when I do go, it always happens sometime between when I get back and dawn. I'm a very early riser, you know," he leans in, grinning flirtatiously. "Always have been."

"I bet you are," I smile back warmly. "But I think it's pretty clear that whatever is pooping on your lawn is not Princess. Her poop looks nothing like the turds on your grass. And I think you can see that now," I add gently.

"Well, maybe," he grumbles. "But then, what's pooping on my lawn every night?"

"My best guess is raccoons," I answer. "Have you seen any around here?"

"Now that you mention it, I do see them from time to time. But they've never bothered me, so I don't bother them."

"Well, it looks like they are bothering you, by using your lawn as a toilet."

"Yeah, I suppose. Well, fine, I suppose you win this round Mae!" He shouts at his neighbor before shuffling back out of the gate. "Just keep your rat on your side of the fence!"

"She's never been on your side, you old codger!" The woman shouts back, triumphant. "And you just admitted it. Hah!"

In the end it isn't exactly a happy resolution, more of a begrudging acceptance, but I get Mr. Fredricks to admit the offending poop isn't from his neighbor's dog, and I get Mrs. Angleton to agree not to leave Princess outside barking for the sake of her neighbors.

When we're back in the car and driving home, Roxanne smiles. "How do you feel that went?"

I shrug. "Pretty good, I guess. I don't think there was a better option, but I suppose you're about to tell me what I could have done better."

"Nope, you're right. I think you found the perfect solution. My guess is that the barking bothers him more than the poop, and it was just an excuse to have a valid complaint. If she sticks to her side of the agreement and limits the barking, I suspect they'll get along fine from here on out. Great job."

Pride swells in my chest at the praise. "Thank you. Now, please tell me there are concerns I'll face that aren't feces-related?"

Chapter Eleven

JARED

~

Sweat keeps building in my palms, and I wipe it on my pants for the fifteenth time before I finally work up the courage to hit 'dial' on my phone.

It's late, and I can't relax. The stress is eating me alive, so I decide to suck it up and do what needs to be done.

It only rings twice before she answers. "Hello?" Her voice is hesitant.

"Hey, Layla. It's me. Jared." Lordy, I sound like a moron.

"Yeah, I know. What's up? Is everything okay?"

"Yes. Well, no." I release the breath I've been holding and start again. "There's nothing for you to worry about, but I needed to talk to you."

"Okay…"

"I'm sorry. For being a jerk earlier."

"Oh. It's okay." Her voice is faint, barely a whisper.

"No, it's not okay. You told me you wanted to deal with it your own way, and I still interfered. And got jealous. And was angry at you for no good reason. It wasn't fair, and I'm sorry."

There's a painfully long pause, and I swear if sweating bullets was an actual thing, I'd definitely be doing that right now because my shirt is soaked.

She sighs. "You're right, it was unfair. But I do appreciate that you called to apologize. Landon and Milo explained that you sometimes get… protective, and you already told me how you felt about Derrek. But you're not the only person with feelings, Jared."

"I know." I swallow hard, and my tone is glum.

But she's not done letting me have it, apparently. "My feelings are every bit as valid as yours, and I'm allowed to feel how I feel about people, your 'protectiveness' aside."

"You're right." *Here it comes.*

"So I think what we need to do is spend more time together."

That gets my attention. "What?"

"You and I haven't had a real chance to hang out, and aside from cheesy jokes and your generosity in delivering me coffee, I don't know much about you besides football."

"I know," I sigh again, defeated. "My schedule is so tight, I swear it's not an excuse! But I have to keep my grades up to stay on the football team, so if I'm not at practice, I'm usually trying to catch up on studying."

"Milo mentioned you're free on Sundays."

"Oh, yeah, right. I usually am." I make a mental note to thank him as soon as I get off this call.

"Why don't you bring your books up here Sunday? We'll get our work done and hang out, and you can have family dinner with me. I'm sure Roxanne would love it."

Excitement spreads through my body, chasing away the anxiety of a few moments before. "Yeah, that sounds great, gorgeous. I'll be there."

She sounds a lot more friendly as we chat for a few more minutes before hanging up, and the tight ball of tension in my chest releases completely.

I'm not out of the woods yet, but I have to keep my jealousy tamped down when it comes to the new professor.

No matter what.

≈

Layla

≈

Thursday at lunch, the guys and I are just hanging out in the SFC cafeteria. Milo and Jared don't have an afternoon class, and Landon and I have nothing until Bio at one. The rest of our friends are chattering around us, and I'm not really paying attention until everyone suddenly stops talking and stares over my head.

Trying out my new skills, I reach out with my senses and feel several individuals who are riddled with nervous energy behind me. I turn, and to my surprise, I face Amber, her two female cronies, and the Westley twins.

Tension is thick in the air, and my supporters glare at the newcomers with clear derision.

Amber and her friends aren't hostile, so I try to remain calm, and wait for someone to speak.

Amber clutches her tray and draws in a deep, steadying breath. "Hi, Layla."

"Hi, Amber."

"Um, I just wanted to say no hard feelings. About the wolf challenge thing, I mean. You're the alpha, and I one-hundred percent respect that."

"Thank you," I reply cooly. If this is her idea of making amends, it leaves a good deal to be desired.

"Also," she swallows, "I'm sorry. For being such a bitch to you when you first got here. I... well, I love my dad, and because of your mom, the whole thing is... kind of complicated," she finishes lamely. "But I shouldn't have treated you that way, regardless. So, I'm sorry."

"Yeah, me too," one of the twins pipes up.

All the others mutter apologies, and I tamp down the intense need to absolve them completely of guilt. It's not my job to make them feel better, and they were jerks.

"Thank you," I answer instead. "Apology accepted."

An obvious wave of relief crosses their faces, and I have to wonder how much of this is just pressure they felt to make up with me, now that I'm alpha.

"Well, that's... all I wanted to say, I guess. I'll see you in bio?"

I nod, and she starts to walk off, but I can't quite believe my own ears when I ask, "Do you want to eat with us?"

I swear her eyes actually light up when she whips around, and the five of them swiftly settle into seats at our table. They begin eating and trying to chat with my steadfast supporters, who are less welcoming than I had been.

"What are you doing?" Jared hisses in a low voice. "She labeled herself your enemy on day one. Are you really going to just forgive her like that?"

I shrug. "She apologized, and I think she was honestly in a tough position. Besides, I don't sense any duplicity from her. She was sincerely apologizing."

"Well, I don't trust it," he murmurs, and the other guys nod in agreement. "Don't forget who she is. She's always up to something. It'd be smart to keep your guard up around her."

"Thank you for the *advice*," I reply sharply in a low voice. "I will keep it under advisement, so long as you remember who *I* am."

His expression immediately tightens. "I'm sorry, you're right. You do you."

I turn my focus to my food, not really up to conversing with the guys at the moment.

Seriously, I have alpha instincts that tell me what people are feeling now. They know this; they grew up in this world. I've only been here a couple of months and I'm already getting the hang of it, so why do they keep insisting on acting like I can't figure anything out on my own?

A tiny voice in the back of my mind suggests, *maybe they just really care about you.* Maybe they don't want me to be hurt, and they're adjusting to the feelings of the bond, which are still pretty new for them, too.

As alpha, I know I'm supposed to be level-headed and thoughtful, always considerate of other people's feelings and needs, and do my best to take care of them.

As an eighteen-year-old girl who has been thrust into a world of magic and responsibility I didn't know existed, I kind of just want to be allowed to stew selfishly in my own feelings for a while.

I think for a few minutes, then shoot off a text to Roxanne. She answers swiftly, and relief floods through me. Suddenly, the idea of resolving more pack problems seems simpler than dealing with my own fated mates.

Drawing in a deep, steadying breath, I make a point to include Amber and the others in conversation, trying to set the tone for the table. It takes some effort, but by the time we've finished our food, things are mostly relaxed.

When we clean up our trays, I let the guys know Maxwell is picking me up after bio lab today.

"Wait, what? I thought I got to drive you home today?" The disappointment in Landon's tone is unmistakable. "I thought we could hang out a while," he adds more quietly.

"I'm sorry." I try to infuse my tone with remorse, even though I'm secretly sort of relieved. "Alpha duties call." I thread my fingers through his. "The good news is, I get you all to myself for lab today."

A small smile curls his full lips. "Yeah, that's true. And it is a three-hour class. I'm just looking forward to when we can help you with alpha stuff so you don't have to do it all yourself."

We head toward the science building, Amber and the Westley twins following.

The tiny thread of guilt worming its way through my chest won't be ignored. Landon just wants to spend time with me, and I honestly don't *have* to deal with the issue this afternoon. I asked Roxanne for an escape from my own mates, and she provided it.

In my heart of hearts, I know they mean well, and I suppose that is where the guilt comes in. But sometimes a girl just needs to deal with something a lot less complicated than boys and their feelings.

Chapter Twelve

LAYLA

～

Roxanne is waiting for me in the back seat when I meet Maxwell out front.

My eyes meet hers curiously. "We're taking the fancy car today, to meet the complainant? I thought Maxwell was just going to drive me up to Harridan House, and we'd take your car again."

Roxanne smooths a hand over her pants, and I realize with a start she's wearing a sleek pinstripe suit instead of her usual khakis and button-down shirt. To top it off, she's got on two-inch stiletto heels. "Part of tending to the pack is understanding the needs and expectations of everyone we're dealing with. The people we met yesterday are simple, humble folk who would have been offended by us driving up in this car.

But where we're going today... well, we'll just say they aren't humble, and they expect you to have all the trappings of power. Here," she thrusts a duffle bag at me. "I packed you something to change into. Campus wear will not cut it today, I'm afraid."

I glance uncomfortably toward Maxwell—I don't relish the idea of changing in full view of his rearview mirror—but he's already raised a dark glass divider between us. Sighing, I dig in the bag and pull out an outfit remarkably similar to Roxanne's. It's a pantsuit with a silky blouse, complete with shiny low heels.

The back seat isn't exactly the size of my closet, but I manage to get the ensemble on during the drive. When I settle back into my seat, a glance out the window tells me we're in an area of town I've never seen. We're cruising slowly along a smooth, recently paved road, and the landscaping to either side is neat and park-like, almost like a golf course, but I don't see anything resembling a fairway.

"Roxanne, who are we meeting, and what is their issue?" A heavy sense of foreboding settles in my stomach. Somehow, I know this will not be a simple complaint about dog poop.

"It's about the property of Peter Jean-Yves," she replies cooly. "Several of his neighbors have accused him of encroaching on their property and attempting to claim it as his own. I've already done the legwork. I have the map of property lines here, so we're basically issuing a cease-and-desist."

"Peter Jean-Yves, as in Amber's dad? One of my mom's rejected?"

"Yes, that's him."

"Jared said... well, he said you told him Peter used to be really nice, before my mom left. And now he's... different. Is that true?"

"Unfortunately, it is. The rejection definitely changed him, and not for the better. He was alway fun-loving, good-natured, and kind. After your mother left, he turned rather bitter. He's been a thorn in your uncle's side for years, and now, unfortunately, the task of dealing with him has come to you."

"So what am I supposed to do? Just tell him to cut it out?"

Roxanne sighs heavily. "Ideally, we'd arrive, he'd greet us kindly, and in a very civilized conversation, we'd explain that he's *mistakenly* claimed some land that isn't his. We'd show him the property line, he'd apologize and that would be it.

"However, don't expect it to go exactly that way. I'd expect that he will be hostile, and there's really no telling how he's going to react to seeing you up close and in person. He was, truly, in love with your mother, and you look just like her. It may have some... unexpected consequences."

I gulp down the lump in my throat. "And do you believe that the property issue is a mistake?"

She snorts. "Not in your life. He's been trying to take more than his share ever since your mother left. I have wondered if it's a direct effect of him being rejected by an alpha... he still innately believes he's entitled to more than the average pack member.

"In theory, everyone in the pack receives the same treatment, everyone is looked after. But we don't prevent people from creating businesses, earning their own keep, and passing down wealth. So, naturally there are some people who are better off than others, just like any society. We don't force communal sharing, but we do charge an income-based tithe to help ensure the communal property is taken care of, streets are paved, and those in the pack with lesser circumstances have everything they need."

"And part of that communal property is Harridan House," I add, following along. "So people like the Jean-Yves family pay a lot to support the alpha, including the work on the grounds, the staff, every-thing." Guilt swamps my chest, thinking of the two older people yesterday in their humble houses, giving money to put me up in a castle.

"Yes, a portion of their tithe goes to the alpha, which has been the same way for centuries," Roxanne replies gently. "No one resents that, Layla. Please try to under-stand—people love the alpha. They want to do their part because the alpha protects us all. The magic in your veins sustains everyone in this town. I know you haven't had a chance to really experience it yet, but you'll see at the Homecoming festivities. Everyone is truly happy you're here."

"Doesn't sound like everyone is," I mutter under my breath.

"Well, it has been a rough time for the pack since your mom left. It's not just about you. Your uncle did his best, but he didn't have a tenth of the strength you have. It was harder for him to bring everyone together, to keep the peace, and make people feel protected. When they don't trust that the alpha can protect them, they take measures into their own hands and become suspicious of others, which leads to more conflict." She pats my hand and gives me a reassuring smile. "As you take more control, show up more in public places and resolve issues, and yes, some of the smiling and waving and baby-kissing political-type stuff, you'll see that things improve drastically. For everyone."

"But not for me," I disagree. "I will always bear the weight of the curse that ties me to this land and prevents me from going anywhere."

Roxanne's encouraging smile drops. "I'm sorry, Layla. I know it's a heavy price to pay. If I had a solution for you, I'd have already taken care of it myself. But there's nothing to be done. People in the Montrose Pack are bitter and spiteful, and there's no reason for us to believe that has changed since they set the curse on us."

"But-"

"We'll have to table this conversation. We're here," Roxanne cuts me off as the car slows, and we pull into a wide, circular drive that curves around an ornate fountain.

When we hop out of the car, I can see the house is massive and covered in stone reminiscent of Harridan

House. Of course, it's much smaller, but I can tell there was deliberate intent in the design. This man seems to have been living in the past ever since my mom left two decades ago.

Swallowing down my nerves, I take my place beside Roxanne, and we march up the stone steps.

"Remember, you are the *alpha*," she whispers. "The ideal solution is that everything goes smoothly, and he complies willingly. But as alpha, you must be willing to assert yourself and force him to comply, for the good of the pack."

"Right, for the good of the pack." I wipe sweaty palms on my pant legs, grateful that the fabric is dark. We've left my wild hair down, and it's suddenly hot on my neck, despite the cool fall weather.

Roxanne gives me one more encouraging smile, then leans forward and pushes the doorbell. Through the frosted glass door, I can see a blurry approaching figure, who turns out to be a butler when the door opens.

"How may I-" he begins in a snooty tone with his nose in the air, then cuts himself off as soon as his eyes land first Roxanne, then me. He steps aside immediately, ushering us inside. "My apologies, alpha, please come in. Are you here to see Mr. Jean-Yves?"

My answer sticks in my throat and my eyes dart to Roxanne, who nods encouragingly. I lift my chin and stride forward. "Yes, I am."

"Right this way to the parlor, and I'll let him know you're here. Can I bring you some refreshments?"

My panicked gaze once again darts to Roxanne. This

time she answers for me. "Yes, refreshments would be lovely, thank you."

We quickly reach a bright room with an enormous fireplace and over-the-top ornate furniture. All of it appears antique, with delicately embroidered cushions I'm terrified to sit on.

Roxanne is nonplussed and claims a seat on the couch, settling into the pillows and crossing her legs at the knees instead of demurely at her ankles like I'm used to. Everything about her exudes an air of power and control, and I try to mimic it. I choose a spot next to her and attempt to position myself comfortably, as if I own the place.

The butler hustles back into the room with a silver tray bearing two glasses of iced tea and some plain-looking shortbread cookies. "Mr. Jean-Yves will be down shortly," he informs us with a grin. A small bead of sweat trails down the side of his bald head, soaking into the collar of his uniform.

Roxanne smiles warmly. "Thank you, Albert. If I may, do you have some of those frosted lemon cookies I had the last time I was here? They were delightful, and I'd love for our alpha to taste one."

Albert positively beams in response. "Absolutely, I'll be right back."

When he bustles off, I glance at Roxanne with one eyebrow raised.

She grins. "His wife is the chef, and she's very proud of those cookies. He is very proud of his *wife*. Part of the job is understanding the people of your pack, and how to make them all feel important and recognized. It doesn't take much."

My head swims. "How am I supposed to remember this stuff about *everyone* in the pack?"

Roxanne claims her glass and takes a sip, waving dismissively. "It'll come naturally to you, I promise. But I'm always here, if you need my help. I've been doing this for a couple of decades now, so I feel pretty confident in saying I've got your back."

Albert returns with a large plate of pale yellow cookies, topped with a thin layer of icing. "Here you are." He places the plate in front of me, and I reach for one and take a bite immediately, playing up the experience of tasting it.

"You're right, they really are delicious." I try to infuse warmth in my praise even though I'm speaking to Roxanne. "Light and crisp, with just the right balance of tart and sweet." Redirecting my attention to Albert, I smile widely. "Thank you, and my compliments to your chef."

His chest puffs with pride. "Thank you, alpha, I will pass those along."

When he leaves again, Roxanne leans in and whispers, "great job," before grabbing a cookie.

"I used to watch a lot of baking shows with my mom," I whisper back.

We munch in silence for a few moments, and I take a sip of the tea—realizing belatedly that its southern-style sweet tea and far too sugary for my taste.

Approaching footsteps reach my ears, and I know

immediately this is not Albert. These footfalls are slow and deliberate, not the light quick step of the butler.

Nerves dance in my stomach—even though I assume he's been at the full moon shifts, I've never met this man officially. After hearing so many things about him, I expect some kind of beast of a man. I try to remember his image in the photos of my mom from when they were young, but all I recall is four skinny kids on the beach, and then in the high school photo, the two boys flanking my mom and dad are complete blanks among the rest of the students.

When he enters, I'm shocked at his appearance. The heavy footfalls led me to believe he was a bigger man, but in fact he's very lean, with an almost hungry look about his pinched face. He's probably close to six feet, rather average looking, aside from the predatory air that surrounds him. The man wears slacks and a button-down shirt, open at the neck, that's pressed neatly and screams 'relaxed professional' even though he's anything but. The energy rolling off of him is dark red and incredibly hostile.

The bite of cookie I just took sticks in my throat, and I gulp down the too-sweet tea to wash it away before I choke. My every instinct warns me not to show weakness in front of this man.

"Alpha, welcome to my humble home," he smiles, gesturing to the surrounding space that is anything but humble. The smile doesn't reach his eyes, and he sits in one of the high-backed chairs facing us. "To what do I own this *honor*?"

The man's eyes are strange. While most people in the pack have something warm in their eyes, as if I can almost sort of see the wolf inside, there is nothing of that in Peter Jean-Yves. His eyes are cold and hard like ice-blue stones, and the only thing that pops in my head, bizarrely, is 'snake eyes'.

Roxanne replies first. "Thank you, Peter. You know I can never resist dropping by for some of these lemon cookies." I note she uses his first name, refusing him any deference. "We are here because several of your neighbors believe you may be mistaken about your property lines, and asked the alpha to sort it out for them."

"Ah, I see. Well, I don't believe we have an issue." His gaze travels to me, and he stares at me like an animal stalking prey, despite speaking to Roxanne.

I swallow hard, holding his gaze and putting on my best smile. "From what we've found in the city records, it seems to be a valid complaint. Roxanne?"

She pulls a sheaf of papers from her briefcase, laying out several. "Here you can see the property lines as filed with the city. And here," she gestures to an aerial photograph, "you can see the lines overlaid on this image of your property. It's very clear the construction you're doing here and here," she points," goes over your neighbor's property by a good deal."

He looks over the images as if studying them carefully, but I can already sense that he doesn't care. In fact, based on his emotions, he actually seems satisfied about it.

"That may be true, based on the plans filed with the city," he allows. "But my neighbors granted me a verbal easement onto their land. They weren't using it, and given the terrain, the location was better suited for my new pool and stables, respectively."

"Do you have any sort of written agreement to this effect?" I ask with as much restraint as I can muster. He knows he's lying directly to my face, and his smug smirk tells me as much.

His answer comes out slowly, as if he thinks I'm too stupid to keep up. "No, as I said, it was a *verbal* agreement. However, I promised them use of both as a concession to the easement."

"Well, unfortunately, they are both complaining about your projects, and insisting you've done it without their permission. So it appears you were mistaken about their agreement with your plans." I don't know where this smooth, lawyerly talk is coming from, but it feels right, so I keep going with it. Perhaps Roxanne was correct about my instincts.

"People often change their minds after making promises," he replies dismissively. "That doesn't change the reality, or the consequences. I'm sure if we have a conversation, I could help remind them of our agreement."

The way he says it brings to mind the sort of tactics a mafia boss would use to get someone to agree to what they want, like busting kneecaps. My blood flows hot in my veins, and I struggle to contain it. "I think not. Regardless of what sort of arrangement you *believed* you had, there is nothing filed with the city office, and nothing in writing to the effect of allowing you to take that land from your neighbors. As they clearly are not in agreement now, I will have to ask you to adjust your plans and move your construction fully onto your property. You have enough to accommodate both facilities easily."

"No, I don't think I will." Peter levels his gaze at me, a direct challenge that raises my hackles. "I'll have a discussion with my neighbors and sort it out. There's no need for your concern, *alpha*."

A fiery ball of power rises in my chest at his condescending tone. I resist the urge to stand for emphasis, and instead level him with my steeliest stare when I tap into the double-timbre of the alpha voice. It resonates in my chest as I speak, causing an odd vibration in my ears.

"Since you are leaving me no choice, I am *ordering* you to stop construction at once, and move your projects so they are completely on your land, with at least a ten-foot distance from your property line so as not to disturb your neighbors further. In addition, I am *commanding* you to restore your neighbors' property to its original state, and you will not speak to them about this matter again. My decision is *final*. Do we have an understanding?"

Peter Jean-Yves glares at me with his pale blue eyes practically bulging from their sockets. A dark red flush creeps up his cheeks, and the fury within him grows even hotter. I can tell he's trying to fight the alpha command; he's not breathing, and his entire body is clenched so tightly he's shaking. I hold his gaze, refusing to blink, and wait for him to comply. It's a battle of wills, even with the alpha command, but I will win.

Eventually he blows out a heavy breath and draws in a strangled gasp, some of the red fading from his face. "Yes, alpha," he replies, bowing his head in submission. "It will be as you command."

I grab another cookie from the plate and lean back in my seat as casually as I'm able, with my heart about to pound out of my chest. "Wonderful. I'm glad we could come to an agreement." I take my time finishing the pastry, watching the man across from me grow more indignant while having absolutely no agency in his own home.

Finally, I rise, brushing crumbs from my lap onto his likely expensive carpet, and Roxanne stands beside me. "Thank you for your hospitality, it was lovely to meet you. We'll leave the maps with you, so you can ensure your projects remain on the correct side of the property lines from here on out."

"Yes alpha," he says again, the barely restrained fury making his voice shake. Apparently not trusting himself to say anything else, he doesn't speak again.

When Roxanne and I emerge from the sitting room, Albert bustles up to see us out, carrying a small tin in his gloved hand.

"Alpha, the chef wanted you to have some cookies to take home with you, with her compliments." His cheeks are flushed, and when he smiles, it's with genuine warmth.

"Thank you, Albert." I accept the tin and grin widely. "I will have to hide these in my room to make sure they last more than a day. My fated can put away cookies like nobody's business."

He chuckles lightly. "Well, if you ever need a refill, just let me know. We would be delighted."

I thank him again, then follow Roxanne outside to the waiting car. I don't draw in a full breath until the doors are closed and we're driving away.

"Great job." Roxanne beams at me, patting my knee. "You handled that very well. How do you feel?"

"Aside from the aftermath of the adrenaline spike, I don't feel too different." I shrug, my heart rate slowly returning to normal. "Tired a bit, I guess? Maybe more like… sort of drained."

"That's from using the compulsion." She nods sagely. "It'll take a while to get used to, like strength-ening a muscle. And it will draw on your magic every time he tries to test it."

"Test it? Test it how?"

"Well, your order forced him to agree. But there are several steps he has to complete, and he will balk at every one. So when he does, your magic will force him to comply. It will pull on you when that happens."

"Now I get what my uncle meant," I murmur. "He said he was expending a lot of energy keeping the town in line. I didn't really understand at the time."

"Yes, because he was not the intended alpha and

people were worried, he had less ability to coax them into complying and ended up using compulsion a good deal. Therefore, it's important for you to determine which situations you can reach an amicable agreement, and which you have no choice but to compel."

I don't really have anything more to say after that, so I relax against the leather seat and watch the scenery go by in silence.

Chapter Thirteen

LAYLA

~

Friday has finally come—I swear this week has been the longest I've ever lived through, attack included—and I'm counting down the hours until I'm finished with classes for the day. After lunch I dart into the ladies' room on my way to the library—I have a free hour before Lit and am planning to do some reading.

I don't realize someone else has followed me until I'm heading for a stall and the door swings open... and I'm suddenly alone with Amber.

Almost instinctually, I reach out with my feelings and validate that she's not planning to attack me. I want to trust her, but I know better than to let my guard down.

Her energy is mostly nervous, and a good deal

scared. Instantly, my instinct to protect kicks in and my initial shock at her appearance warms. "Hey Amber," I say casually, then wait to see if she has something to say. We just had lunch at the same table and she didn't give me any indication that she wanted to speak to me, but that doesn't mean much.

It's also entirely possible that she's upset about something personal and has no intention of telling me about it.

But the way she's standing, awkwardly watching me in the bathroom, makes me pause.

She doesn't look like the same put-together, self-assured princess I met on my first day at Smoky Falls College. Dark circles hang under her eyes, and instead of polished, she just appears... disheveled and tired.

But still, she just looks at me nervously and fidgets.

"Are you okay?" I prompt, resisting the urge to cross my hands over my chest. I want her to tell me whatever is on her mind, and I know that movement will just come across as defensive. With our history, I want her to know I'm not holding grudges.

"You were at my house yesterday."

"Yes, I was." Is this about some kind of revenge for her father?

"My dad was... really angry." Her eyes are glossy with unshed tears, and my heart lurches.

"I'm sorry if that upset you. I didn't want to use compulsion on him, but he left me no choice."

"No, it's not that," she sniffles, wiping at her eyes with the sleeve of a sweater. "He knows what he does is wrong, but he always justifies it to himself. I don't blame you for what you did. I swear."

"Okay…" I wait for her to speak again, wishing I could dive into her brain without having to force her to tell me.

"He… well before you came back, he was angry that Lilliana Harridan rejected him, forcing him to choose a different mate. But I think he sort of saw me as his opportunity to correct it, I guess. I grew up under the expectation that I would become alpha some day."

"I'm sorry. I didn't come here to take something away from you. I didn't even know what this place was, or who I was."

"No, you don't understand," she emits a half-sob of a laugh. "I'm terrible at explaining this. I'm not mad you came back. I'm *grateful*. I didn't want any of it. It felt unnatural, wrong, and I grew up believing I didn't have a choice. So I tried to be what they told me I had to be, and when you beat me at the challenge, I was *relieved*. Just like I was relieved that you told him to stop with the construction. Our neighbors are nice people, and I hate everyone thinking I'm an entitled brat because of how my dad acts.

"But you should know, when you do those things, there are consequences." Her voice grows shaky at the end, and I can see now that she is literally trembling.

"Amber, what do you mean *consequences*?" I try to keep my tone light, but I can already see the writing on the wall. Her fear is not about me.

"When dad doesn't get his way, he… he takes it out

135

on my mom. And me. Because we aren't ever good enough," she replies in a near-whisper.

It takes every ounce of my self-control to hold in the roar of fury I want to release. I knew he was a shitty human, but I had no idea he was abusive toward his family. The need to protect bubbles under my skin, white-hot rage for the person responsible. I want to shred him to pieces with my bare hands.

Instead, I tamp it down—I can tell Amber has been traumatized enough—and reach out to her as slowly and gently as I'm able, wrapping an arm lightly around her shoulders.

"Amber, I'm sorry. I had no idea that is how he would react. Have you ever told someone before? I can't imagine my uncle Dom would have let him carry on behaving that way."

She shakes her head. "No, he forbade us from speaking to Dom because he said he wasn't truly the alpha. My mom was too afraid. So we didn't really have anywhere else to go for help. But now... I mean, you're here, you're the *alpha*, and I thought... maybe you'd have a solution."

And suddenly, I get it. *This* is what Roxanne meant, that the pack didn't have trust in my uncle, so he couldn't protect them. Not even from their own families.

"You bet I do," I reply firmly. "I'm going straight over to your house and forbidding him from ever laying a hand on you or your mom again."

"No, you can't!" She pulls away, shaking her head

with wide, terrified eyes. "I don't know what he'll do if he knows I told you."

"What does it matter? He can't disobey the alpha command, so you'll be safe."

"It's more than that. They want you *dead*. My dad and his friends have been trying to come up with a way to take you out since you arrived. Their goal is to kill you before the eclipse, so you never fully claim the seat as alpha."

"Don't they understand that my blood is tied to a spell protecting this place?" I sigh, abruptly weary. "I don't *want* to be alpha any more than they want me to, but I don't have a choice, apparently. If a Harridan isn't alpha, it breaks the contract or whatever with the earth magic and this will no longer be a magically protected place." I think I've gotten the gist of it, even if I've left out some details.

"Well, that's the thing; because of my dad's bloodlines, combined with my mom's, I've probably got the most second-most Harridan blood in the pack. They think that's enough to keep the magic going."

"Wait, so they're *still* planning on trying to force you to be alpha?" My anger resurfaces. "And you told them you don't want it?"

"My dad doesn't care what I want. I think it's always been about getting revenge on your mom. I'd bet he pounced on my mom so quickly after yours left because she had no fated and had so much Harridan blood. In fact... never mind. Just suffice it to say, I think this has been his plan for a long time."

Her abrupt stop in the middle of a sentence gets my suspicion up. "Wait, what were you going to say?"

Amber fidgets with the sleeve of her sweater. "I don't really know anything. It's just a feeling I got."

"I love feelings."

She sighs, tucking a strand of blonde hair behind her ear. "Okay. A couple years ago, my mom admitted to me she had a fated mate—I never knew growing up, I always assumed she was unfated—and he died just days after your mom left. Fell off a cliff while he was hiking with a bunch of friends."

A sick feeling twists in my stomach. "And?"

Amber turns to me with wide eyes. "And something made me wonder if my dad had something to do with it," she admits in a whisper. "He was one of the kids hiking. It seems awfully convenient that he was rejected and she lost her fated just a couple days later, doesn't it? I grew up sort of believing they had their own kind of fated/unfated love story. But the more I think about it, the more I wonder."

My heart is heavy for her. "I'm so sorry, Amber. I'm sorry that this has been your life. It's not fair, and you don't deserve it. Neither does your mom." I pull her into a hug, and the dam breaks, hot tears leaking onto my shoulder as she cries. "I won't go confront your dad just yet. But I'm going to figure out how to get you and your mom out of there, and soon. Okay?"

She nods into my shoulder, then sighs. "He just... can't know I told you. After I failed to beat you in the alpha challenge, he was *furious*."

Anger rises like a wild beast in my chest again, and I suddenly realize Landon was right. It feels like something is trying to claw its way out of my skin, but the casing is too tough for it to get through.

"I promise he won't know," I answer through my teeth. "Can you stay somewhere else? Like over at a friend's house for a while? Maybe under the guise of a sleepover for the weekend?"

"I could probably," Amber answers dubiously. She leans back, wiping her cheeks and gazing at me with pink, tear-filled eyes. "But then I'd be leaving my mom alone with him."

"I understand. Well, do the best you can to avoid him, and I'll get to work on a solution. But I promise I won't do anything without talking to you first, okay?"

"Okay," Amber sniffles. "Thank you, alpha."

"Please, just call me Layla," I reply with a smile. "We're friends, right?"

"Okay, Layla," she smiles back. "Friends."

Chapter Fourteen

LAYLA

〜

I get Amber sorted out and make sure she's ready to her next class before I leave. Then, instead of heading for the library as I'd intended, my feet—for whatever reason—lead me to Derrek's office.

Fortunately, he has office hours Friday afternoons before his last class of the week, and there's not another student talking to him already.

He's leaning over his desk, one hand toying with his curls while he reads. A light knock at his door gets his attention, and he looks up at me in surprise.

"Lex, welcome! I wasn't expecting you. You're not... here to get out of your reading, are you?" His teasing grin tells me he knows that's not the case. I step inside the tiny room as he closes the book he was reading and settles back in his chair. The office is neat, although there's barely room for a desk and chairs. It's nearly empty aside from a few binders and a handful of books on the shelf crammed behind his desk.

"I guess you still need to get unpacked," I comment as I take the vacant seat.

"Yeah, I don't really have much stuff. I travel light. But I suppose now that I'm here, I should start building out my collection. Being a literature professor and all." He grins, green eyes flashing, and I try to tamp down the ripple of excitement that goes through me in response.

"But I'm guessing you're not here to discuss my empty shelves. So what can I do for you, Lex?"

"Honestly, I don't really know why I'm here. I just had an alpha thing come up, but it's not something you can help me with. I was intending to go to the library and just… kind of ended up here."

He nods seriously. "Well, you did always come to me for advice, before. Maybe it's that instinct resurfacing?"

"Maybe."

The silence stretches between us, and my foot twitches nonstop. I know he's waiting for me to spill whatever's bothering me, but I'm not really sure I should trust him with pack business. An electric charge fills the air of the small room, and I rack my brain for something to say.

"How are your lessons going?"

His head tilts to the side. "Lessons, like my classes? Good so far, I guess. No complaints that I'm aware of."

"No, your seer lessons. Roxanne told me you'd have to take some lessons with the pack seer to determine if you have the gift. That's why you're here, right? Because we need a replacement seer?"

"Ah." Derrek's cheeks flush and a distinctly guilty look crosses his expression. "Lex... I think it's time for me to come clean. I need to tell you something, but can you hold off on your judgement until I've told you everything?"

Distrust rises in my chest. With a preface like that, something tells me whatever he has to say, I'm not going to like it. My jaw tightens, but I agree. "Okay, I'll hear you out."

"Um... would you close the door behind you?" He points to the narrow door that's propped open with a hand weight. I have to move my chair to close it and then reclaim my seat.

The space suddenly feels even smaller with the door closed. I clasp my hands in my lap and focus on keeping my expression placid.

Derrek runs his fingers through his hair and mutters something to himself that sounds like 'here goes nothing,' before clearing his throat.

"Okay, so I told you on Monday that I met your uncle in LA at the ER, and he and his witch recognized instantly that I was... not human. That was all true."

He pauses for confirmation, and I nod. I remember that part.

"Okay, so... the rest of it was... not exactly true."

"How? I'm not following what you mean."

"The part about me being related to your seer? I'm not, exactly. I'm more closely related to her relatives, the ones who created the faction and divided the pack."

It takes me a second to take that all in. "You mean the witch who created the *Montrose Pack* and cursed my family line?"

He swallows, the gulp audible in the tiny space. "That's the one. I was part of the Montrose Pack, and I ran away. I didn't want to be part of their politics and their scheming. So I made my way out west, and that's where I met you. And I didn't run into a single soul like us out there."

"But you knew who I was." My tone is flat. My heart rate has been climbing ever since he admitted to lying to me, and the only thing going through my brain is *Jared was right*.

He rushes to explain. "No, I didn't know who you were. You were Layla, then Lex, remember? I learned briefly of the Harridans in my pack, but you never used that name. I didn't know anything about the whole extended history. I could tell you were a wolf, and that you didn't realize it. That's all I knew."

My eyes narrow. "That seems pretty fucking convenient, if you ask me. You expect me to believe that you: ran away from the pack who wants my entire family dead, are even *descended* from the family who cast a curse that my mother ran away from, and just *happened* to find me on the other side of the country?" I can't help reaching out with my instincts, but just as before, I can't really get a handle on his emotions. It makes me feel weak, blind, having to lean on only the visual clues he gives me. It seems I've already become too accustomed to my alpha senses to help me navigate confrontation. "I thought my fated were being paranoid assholes about you. I defended you to them, and now I find out you not only lied to me the entire time I knew you, you popped back into my life like nothing happened in the last year and just kept on *lying*."

I can't remain in my seat any more. I'm furious that I came here on instinct for comfort, both at myself and at him. "I guess the good news is that since I'm the alpha now, I have the authority to get rid of you. I trust I won't need to get our security team involved."

"Wait, Lex, you promised to hear me out." Derrek's face has dropped, his expression desperate. "Just let me finish and then, if you still want me to leave, I'll go. I swear."

My heart clenches at the desperation in his voice, and it combats the waves of fury coursing through my blood. I glare at him for a moment, then settle stiffly in my chair. "Fine, finish your story."

"Okay," the hand goes through his hair again, and he paces behind his desk. "So, I ran away when I realized I could never be what my pack wanted. My mom was the pack witch, but I had next to no magic, and no siblings. Somehow she shielded me from their expectations, and I didn't know they thought I was pursuing my education with the plan to return eventually and take my mother's place. As much as I loved my mom, I didn't want that life, nor did I have the power to be what they expected. The pack paid for my education, you understand? Sure, I got some scholarships, but they thought they were educating me in return for my future services. My mom... well, I guess she felt the pack owed her more than she had received, so she deceived us all."

"Wait," I can't help but interrupt. "So you were allowed to attend school away from the pack?"

"Well, yeah. You have to remember, the restrictions on Smoky Falls are... unique. Based entirely on the issues that arise from the curse. At my former pack, we were free to come and go as we pleased. The magic enables shifting on pack land, but there's not the same sort of... compulsion to do it you have here. At least, as far as I understand. I'm still learning."

My red-hot fury becomes molten, like lava in my gut. My pack's existence is so difficult because of them, and they share *none* of the consequences. "Go on," I spit from between clenched teeth.

"So anyway, my mom finally told me the truth. I freaked out and ran away from the responsibility before they could catch on. I ended up in LA, and you know all that happened after that, until the night you were attacked. Your uncle knew right away I was not human, and his witch could sense magic on me. They didn't tell me where they were from or what they knew, but basically they said enough to get me to confess who I was. I'm also part wolf, you understand. My dad was a member of the pack, my mom their witch. So I have both of them in my blood, and none of their gifts. It is an odd combination."

"Wait, you're also half *wolf*? But you said you have none of your father's gifts... does that mean you can't shift?"

"That's what my mom told me. To be honest, I never tried. It was like a dirty secret. I got the impression she had an affair with a member of the pack. The official story was that my dad was some human, an outsider, but once I learned the truth, it all made a ton more sense.

"So, once we figured out I couldn't really work earth magic, we moved to a neighboring town to keep it secret, and she commuted to Montrose for work every day. She told the pack she wanted to raise me among the humans so I could get a break from the magic in between working spells. The truth is, I could do some tiny spells if I spent a ton of energy to make them happen. My mom supplemented me a good deal, trying to encourage me. Like making me believe I had powers would make them manifest." He snorts in derision.

"But anyway, your uncle figured out who I was, and offered me the position here. He promised to keep my lineage a secret, with the cover story of being related to the seer to answer questions that came up."

"Why, though?"

Derrek seems relieved to have finished his story, and sits down. "Why what?"

"Why did my uncle do that? The part I don't get is

why, after finding out you're a runaway from the pack who cursed us, actually related to the witch who cast the spell—why would he invite you here, and give you a place to stay, a job?"

"I don't know for certain, but he said a few things to me over the course of a year that made me suspect he had a plan. I reached out to some family that I trusted, and I think your uncle was on to something before he disappeared."

"And what's that?"

"I think your uncle was looking for a way to break the curse."

The suspicion and derision drain from my body in an instant, electric tingles racing over my skin. "Why do you think so?"

"Your uncle asked a lot of questions about my bloodlines, my family, the Montrose Pack structure. I told him everything I knew, and I think he had a contact within that pack. But he seemed interested in my family, the magic they practiced, and the pack blood-lines. It didn't mean much to me until I found out about the Smoky Falls curse and how it came to be. And that's when I realized it."

"Realized what?" I'm breathless now. As if we'd been of the same mind without even knowing, Derrek and I were on a similar path of discovery all along.

He leans forward, eyes alight with excitement. "I think the way to break the curse is to recombine the packs."

Chapter Fifteen

LAYLA

~

"Well, he's completely off his rocker," Landon snorts. We're at Badger's, having an early dinner after class.

"Told you I didn't like him," Jared agrees with an air of vindication. "I *never* trusted him, and turns out my instincts were correct. So, did you banish him from pack lands?"

"Not exactly," I hedge. In fact, Derrek and I talked a good deal more, right until class started. And by the end, I forgave him for concealing his identity from me.

"Are you kidding?" Jared is incredulous. "He's from *Montrose*, and the whole lot of them are traitors."

"Well, I understand his logic in not revealing his history to me back in LA, and he had an agreement with my uncle to protect his cover story. To be fair, he didn't even keep that promise a week before he confessed, guys. And… I know it's hard for you to understand, but even though I can't use alpha senses on him, I still don't feel like he's trying to hurt me." The truth I don't reveal is that Derrek is feeling more and more important to me with every minute I spend in his presence, and I still don't know what it means.

Milo hasn't spoken for an extended period, thoughtfully chewing his food and listening to the three of us. "I think it comes down to whether or not we trust Lex. I trust her to do what's right for the pack, period."

I beam at him gratefully, but his next statement swiftly sours my generous feelings.

"However, just because he's not actively trying to harm anyone doesn't mean he's *right*. Our pack has been under this curse for decades. Surely if there was a solution to it, someone would have found it by now. And no offense, Lex, but your uncle wasn't exactly the strongest alpha to ever run our pack. I can understand him being desperate to get out of the curse, especially when you've already proven to be ten times the alpha that he was, and not even half his age."

"Exactly," Jared leans back in his seat. "I couldn't have said it better myself."

My excitement drops and my eyes shift to Landon. "So you really don't think it could be real, either?"

His soulful brown eyes are filled with sadness. "Layla, you know I want more than anything for it to be true. But it's just hard to trust it right now. There's no need for us to decide anything today. We can take our time and figure it all out, right?"

I nod in agreement, sighing. I'd been so excited, talking with Derrek, about the prospect of breaking the curse. Even though everyone was resistant to the idea that it could be done, it pisses me off that they just straight up believe it's *impossible*. Even my fated mates, who are meant to support me in every endeavor, talk around it. Like it's so cute that I believe this fairy tale, but I'm living in a fantasy world and I need to grow up.

"Come on." Milo throws a comforting arm around me and pokes me in the ribs, drawing a surprised laugh from my lips. "Tonight is about having fun and reclaiming our lost youth."

"Hey speak for yourself, old man. I very much still consider myself youth," Jared retorts.

"By all means, Homecoming King," Landon snorts. "Let's go visit the site of your crowning glory."

The guys convinced me to go to the local high school football game tonight—they have their homecoming festivities the week before the college holds theirs. Even though it all bleeds into a giant town celebration, Smoky Falls at least tries to give the high schoolers as normal of an experience as they can. They'll apparently have a dance tomorrow in the school gym.

I'm looking forward to the game. Now that I understand the rules a little better, of course. And Jared will be with us in the stands, so it's more time with him, too.

Plus, the weather is much cooler and I don't have to worry about dying of heat stroke.

Jared assures me the entire town will be out for the game, and he's not wrong. We leave Landon's SUV parked at the restaurant and join the mass of people walking down the main strip toward the high school.

Of course, we have to stop at the Painted Moose because Milo needs his java fix, and he picks up hot cocoa for the rest of us from a tent set up outside for the very purpose. True to my fated's assurances, there's a festive atmosphere running through the entire town. Everyone is bundled in jeans and fall jackets, cheeks rosy from the cool breeze, and the crisp scent of apples and bonfire floats in the air.

And everywhere I look, people are beaming in my direction. They catch my eye and wave like they just spotted a celebrity. At first it's a little disconcerting, but as I tap into my alpha senses, I start to see what Roxanne means. They're genuinely happy to see me; the smiles aren't duplicitous, and I feel almost buoyed up by the wave of excitement. If my fated give me electric tingles from contact, it almost feels like just being around the pack is a subtle source of power to me.

We follow the crowd flooding into the high school football field and claim seats a few rows up from the grass. I'm surrounded by my fated—Landon even brought a blanket to warm our laps—and I'm cozy despite the chill.

And I get it. I really, truly *get it*. The pack is one giant family of sorts, they've got this little piece of the good life—the apple cider and fall bonfires, the joy of knowing your kids will stay and raise their families just down the street, sending their kids to the same schools you went to—and the cycle will continue.

My presence, my family and our sacrifice, ensures that. The guys, taking their places as my mates and future alphas, ensure that. It's one driving purpose that keeps the entire world (as they see it) spinning.

But I didn't grow up in this world. The world I know is different, and yes, perhaps some of it was pretty terrible, but this safe little existence is rife with a very small town attitude. One that screams, *this is the best we're going to get, so we'll make the most of it and hold on like hell to every little scrap of happy we can get.*

And a fierce, fiery little part of me shouts to be heard inside my mind. *What if I'm here to* break *the cycle? What if my purpose here is to break the curse and free them all from the oppression they've accepted, they even believe is something they want?*

I smile and sip my cocoa, watching the band play and the cheerleaders cheer. When Jared is called to crown the new homecoming king along with Amber, who crowns the queen, I stand and cheer with the rest of them. We watch the game together, and Jared slips me laffy taffy's from a giant bag in his coat pocket. I do my part and return the wrappers to him so he can record the jokes.

But beneath the surface, I'm chewing over everything I've been told since arriving at Smoky Falls, and wondering just how deep their innate bias colors their 'truth'.

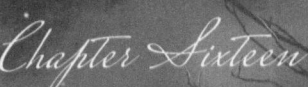

Chapter Sixteen

LAYLA

Saturday, Jared has an out-of-town football game, and I tell Landon and Milo that I need time to catch up on my homework.

In reality, I spend the entire day pouring through volumes in the library, trying to find more information about my ancestors and the curse. I locate my great grandmother's diaries, and I even find the one that begins with her taking over as alpha at fifteen and being forced to claim two more mates.

It's not what I hoped for, but probably about as much as I expected.

She was angry; resentful at having to take on a responsibility she didn't believe was hers, furious at the separatists who left and killed her sister.

I skim through several books, but they mostly detail her extreme reactions to shoring up what she saw as weaknesses in their defenses.

And so it all came down to the Harridans, once again. Because my great grandmother became a fearful, bitter woman, and she shaped the pack to be fearful and bitter as well.

Following in her footsteps, my grandmother held the same policies, the same beliefs, the same iron grip on the pack.

And then there was my mom, who refused. She left, forcing my uncle to take on the role when he was too weak to hold it, and things began crumbling around the edges.

Which leads us to me.

By the early evening, I'm exhausted and re-shelving dozens of books. I don't want to leave the mess for someone else to clean up, and I certainly don't want them to suspect my motives.

The last thing I need tonight is another lecture from Mr. Carson about my duties to the pack.

In truth, I'm sick to *death* of everyone telling me what I need to do. They've grown up with the long-held beliefs in what keeps them safe and protects them. I've come in with none of those biases, and my perspective is vastly different.

Does that mean I'm right? I have no way of knowing. But it certainly feels like every fiber of my being is telling me I have to at least try to change things for the better. Because nothing will change if you continue doing the same thing over and over again. They may have convinced themselves that they're content with the way things are, but I think about what Derrek said, how people in Pack Montrose come and go, returning occasionally to reconnect with the pack but not forced to be there.

A cold, hard stone of resolve settles in my gut.

Someone, somewhere, knows the truth about all of this.

And I intend to find them.

Jared shows up Sunday just after breakfast for our study/hangout date, wearing jeans and a thick hoodie, looking every part the college football hunk complete with flat-brim baseball cap. His rich brown skin contrasts beautifully with the pale color of his SFC shirt and matching cap. I can tell he's nervous, because he opens with a joke.

"Hey gorgeous, what kind of bow loves water?" He greets me in the foyer with a hug and presses a kiss to my temple, sending electric tingles down my body.

"I dunno, Jared, what kind?"

"A *rain*bow." His grin widens when I groan.

"Okay, I think you used up all your best material early on. They're definitely getting worse," I tease him as we trudge upstairs to my suite. He drops his backpack on the floor with a heavy thud.

"How much reading do you need to do?" I ask, one eyebrow raised.

"A lot," he sighs, throwing his head back. "I was gone from eight in the morning until past ten last night. They wanted to do some kind of team-building thing before the game. Don't get me wrong, paintball is fun, but I would rather have had the sleep."

"I don't blame you. The football schedule is pretty intense. But you love playing, right?"

"Yeah, I do," he answers, but he doesn't sound so sure.

"I sense a 'but' somewhere in there," I prod.

"Well, it's just kind of pointless, isn't it?"

"What do you mean?"

"It's fun now, but it's not like it's going to lead to a career. I can't join the NFL or something, you know what I mean?"

My heart lurches for him. "Okay, I get that. But you've known that all along, right? And there are other things you can do, I'm sure."

"Like become a coach?" He snorts. "I suppose. Not my ideal career choice."

"And it's not worth playing, just to play?"

"I don't know how to explain it. I've known the limitations that come with the pack from day one, and I understand them. We have to be close by. And it's not like we could take all the blood tests and everything else with our freaky wolf blood. There's no way we'd pass for human.

"I see guys I've played against since we were in

junior league posting about scholarships to Notre Dame or Big Ten schools, getting recruited to go play places that lead to careers. And I have better stats. I *know* I'm a better player, and I have every right to those same opportunities.

"Buuut... I have to stay here. Attend Smoky Falls College, graduate with an associate's degree—probably in physical education—and if I'm lucky finish out my degree at a school in North Carolina or here in Tennessee, so I'm close enough to drive home every month for the shift. It's just... sad to think about it sometimes."

"You realize you're preaching to the choir, right?" I elbow him in the ribs, trying to show him I relate, but also lighten the mood. "I'm *literally* stuck here. I can't even leave for over twenty-four hours or I'll apparently drop dead and take the whole town with me."

Jared's eyes widen with embarrassment. "Gorgeous, I'm so sorry. I completely forgot. Here I'm whining about Notre Dame. I'm an idiot. My only defense is that I'm too tired to think straight, clearly."

"It's fine, I really get it. I had some pretty big dreams before landing here and finding out I was *literally* cursed."

"Oh yeah? Like what?"

Bright light is streaming into my little suite—it's a beautiful fall day outside. I hesitate to answer him, and I realize it's because I'm worried about being overheard.

"You know what? Let's get outside, go for a walk.

It'll be refreshing and hopefully give us some energy before we tackle homework."

Jared shrugs. "Sounds good to me."

He's already dressed for the cooler weather, so I pull on a thick fleece hoodie and we head outside, following the same path I took the first day I spent at Harridan House, when it was all mysterious and misty.

Now the sky is completely cloudless, and the brilliant blue contrasts against the riot of color from the changing leaves. It's been fun to watch them, see how every day they're a little different, and notice the subtle change as I drive down the mountain to the town where they've only begun to change. Here there's hardly any green left besides the pine trees, and a thick carpet of fallen leaves coats the ground.

We walk in comfortable silence for a while, our breath a light mist in the chilly air. It's not until we descend the second set of steps and are truly in the gardens, away from structures, that I speak.

"You asked what my dreams were, before I became alpha, and the truth is I had nothing specific. I wanted to be happy, I wanted to have a home, and I wanted to travel. I spent my entire life in and around Los Angeles —we never went anywhere. Sure, we took trips to the beach, but we stuck to the Southern California coast line. I didn't have specific plans like, 'I want to go to Harvard,' although I knew I wanted to go to school. I wanted to read a lot. I wanted to travel and see things I'd only seen on tv or the internet."

"I think those are all wonderful dreams, gorgeous."

"Yeah, well, not much I can do about them now, is there? It's not like I can go visit the Eiffel Tower or the pyramids in Egypt with a 24-hour timer around my neck." I try to be light-hearted, but realize I mostly just sound bitter.

"I understand," he replies. "It sucks, all of it. And I think we have every right to be pissed about all the things we can't do."

The hard edge to his tone surprises me. "Really? I thought you were 'Mr. Homecoming King town favorite golden boy star football player.' Everyone loves you here, and you seem... perfectly suited to this place."

"So, because I'm doing okay with the hand I've been dealt, I'm not allowed to dream bigger?" His voice takes on a surprising note of sarcasm. "I've tried to make the best of it, but the truth is, I'm *pissed*. It's not fair that I can't go after the career I want, or travel, or even live where I want. It's not fair that you're stuck here, either. It all sucks, and there's nothing we can do about it. So for the most part, I try to be positive because I have no choice, but sometimes... I don't feel all sunshine and light." He kicks at a rock that's rolled onto the paved path, sending it zooming off into the trees.

I don't need my alpha senses to tell me he's finally being real with me, showing me his true feelings. Warmth spreads through my chest, and I lace my fingers through his.

"Thank you," I murmur, leaning in to his side. "I

can't tell you how crazy I've felt, being here and being so... frustrated that everyone is so stuck in their ways, so biased in their perception of this place, that they can't see all the drawbacks. It's honestly a relief to hear someone else say it."

Jared emits a low chuckle, his hand tightening as he nudges me gently with a muscular shoulder. "It honestly didn't occur to me that, being from the outside, it'd be so much harder for you to adapt. We've been raised with all the limitations of pack life, and it still chafes from time to time, but it's home. I think we've gotten better at tamping down our frustration with it. We assume we'll get over it, settle more, be happier. Or maybe that's just me."

"Hey, let's go this way." I tilt my head toward the side path that leads to the clearing in the woods. "I've never seen it in the daylight."

We veer off and follow the rough trail, sunlight dappling the brightly colored leaves littering the forest floor. The warm electric tingles of being with one of my fated continue to flow over my skin, equal parts comforting and exciting.

As if reading my mind, or perhaps just my mood, Jared speaks. "Layla," his voice is softer, hesitant. "I know I talk a big game, but I... well, I don't really have any more, um... experience than the other guys."

"Okay..." I'm not sure what I'm supposed to reply to that one.

"I just can't really get a read on what you think of me, sometimes," he admits with a heavy sigh. "I feel like of the three of us, you like me the least. I've never felt that way in my entire life. I've never been the last picked for a team, or the person no one wanted to be around. I don't know what I'm doing wrong."

I consider his words for a minute, reaching out with my senses while we walk. The hesitation was clear in his voice, but I can feel the anxiety now, the deep, underlying fear of *not being good enough*. My hand tightens on his thick fingers.

"I agree that you and I haven't been as close as I've become with the others. But it's not about not *liking* you as much. If I'm being really honest, I think it's because I feel you keep me, and everyone else, at arm's length. Landon is very open about his feelings, he practically wears his heart on his sleeve. I know where I stand with him. And Milo is…" I can't help chuckling, "Milo is Milo. He's always been very clear about who he is and what he thinks. But you…"

I tug his hand, pulling him to a stop. We're at the edge of the clearing now, and I need to look him in the eyes for this part. I wait for him to lift his gaze from the leaves beneath our feet, and I reach up to tug off the cap he wears low over his dark eyes before I continue. "You've been different. I feel like… you hide who you are, somehow. Behind the jokes, and the football captain, cool guy persona. It's like a mask you wear, and it's done the job, gotten you the popularity, the admiration from most of the town. You're super good at it. Sometimes it's even hard for me to reach your genuine emotions with my alpha senses.

"But this is the first time you've shown me something *real*; what you really feel, what you *really* think. And I'm willing to bet that *this* is the Jared that Milo and Landon know, the one they keep telling me is there 'once I get to know you'. And this is the Jared I want to know *more*. Because I feel like I've been alone on an island since I arrived here, and you've made me feel more seen in the last ten minutes than I have in two months."

Jared's pulse is racing; I can feel it through our clenched hands, see it throbbing in the vein just below his jaw. Without the hat shading his eyes, sunlight fills his irises and brings out golden flecks I didn't know existed in the dark chocolate brown. His gaze locks on mine, lips parted slightly, and the rushing of blood through my ears drowns out the sounds of the surrounding forest in the indeterminably long moment.

Then, as if time speeds up, Jared drops my hand and his wide, warm fingers cup my face on both sides. In one smooth movement, he's pressed against me and his lips envelop mine, pillow-soft and gentle.

Electricity crackles between us, and I respond by wrapping my arms around his waist and pulling his hard, muscular body even tighter to mine. Heat rolls off him, even through our sweatshirts, and licks at my skin with delicious tingles. I can't resist pulling his lower lip between my teeth and running my tongue along it. Jared responds with a low growl that reverberates deep in my chest, and his hands fall away from my face to grip my body while mine rise, in concert, to circle his shoulders.

Of my three mates, Jared is the closest to my height but also the most muscular. I can't resist running my fingers over his wide shoulders, trailing along the hard muscles of his neck and back while our kisses grow wilder. His warm palms slide along the sides of my body, working their way to my waist, then my hips, before wrapping around my butt and clenching me against him.

The heat and pressure between our hips sends my pulse skyrocketing; tension is coiling in my belly and it's all too much sensation and yet not nearly enough. I pull on his neck as I try to leverage myself higher, and Jared obliges, scooping me up by my backside and taking several steps to press me against a nearby tree. The bark is rough, the tree hard against my back, but now my legs are wrapped around him and the hardness between his hips is exactly where I want it. My hips tilt and move of their own accord, and Jared's move with me, adding to the sensation.

I can scarcely breathe, and I pull back from our frantic kisses to catch my breath. Jared trails hot lips down my neck, along my jaw, to the other side while our bodies continue to move together. I'm practically seated on his lap with the way he has me wedged against this tree, and my fingers scramble to find his warm skin through the open neck of his hoodie.

The nearby crunch of a footstep on leaves causes us

to freeze immediately, both of our heads whipping toward the noise.

Across the clearing, a deer stands at alert with wide, fearful eyes. I can see its nostrils flare as it draws in breath, trying to scent us and figure out if we're dangerous.

A leaf detaches from the tree above us, drifting lazily toward the ground. As if the spell is broken, the deer turns and bolts back into the forest.

Jared and I turn our gazes to each other, and then as one burst out laughing. I tighten my grip around his neck and he steps away from the tree, carefully lowering me to the ground before claiming a few more soft kisses. I run to pick up his hat where I dropped it in the heat of the moment, brushing it off with the sleeve of my hoodie before presenting it to him.

He takes the cap, then sets it on top of my head. It doesn't quite fit over my wild hair, so I loosen the snap back and settle it over my curls with the brim tilted up.

"Approve?" I ask him playfully.

Jared pretends to consider for a moment, then a wide pearly grin splits across his mahogany face. "Gorgeous," he states, drawing me into his body and kissing my cheek from behind. "Come on, gorgeous. I'm starving. Let's go get some lunch."

He wraps his warm hand around mine and tugs me back toward the path that leads home.

Chapter Seventeen

LAYLA

〜

Jared and I spend the whole day together, and eventually we get to our homework.

Not to mention a fair bit more making out under the guise of 'relaxing'.

My lips are tender and swollen when we head downstairs for dinner, and if Roxanne or the staff notice, they don't say a word.

Once he heads home for the night, I take my time getting ready for bed, mooning happily around my rooms as I tidy up. Now that I have my own space, I can't bear for it to be messy, and I know that if I don't clean up the maids will, which needles me even more. I don't want them to think I've become some kind of spoiled princess.

My phone pings, and when I check it, I'm delighted to see it's another audio file from Landon. This one is a wistful song about unrequited love, and my heart squeezes at the plaintive note in his voice.

I reply immediately and send him back heaps of praise. Then I take a moment to send all three of my fated a different selfie, along with a quick note about the unique things I appreciate about each of them.

Jared's words earlier got to me, and I've been chewing on them in the back of my mind ever since. He's not the only one who keeps people at a distance, away from his true self. I know I'm guilty of the same, rarely letting people in.

So I plan to make a conscious effort to show more appreciation for the people around me. Starting with my fated.

A strange urge drives me to pull up a text to Derrek and send him a message as well, but I hesitate with what I should actually say. Obviously not the same things I sent to my fated, but then what?

I type out, then delete several messages, before finally settling on the simplest of all.

I'm glad you're back in my life. I'll see you tomorrow.

I get it sent off before a flood of messages pours in from my fated, praising my photos and thanking me for my messages, then replying with selfies and heartfelt sentiments of their own.

A warm, bubbly feeling takes up residence in my

chest, and it jumps another notch when I receive a reply from Derrek.

There's nowhere I'd rather be. Come see me at office hours tomorrow. I have something to tell you.

Even though I know my focus should be on my classes, or on my fated, my mind is wholly preoccupied with what Derrek wants to see me about today.

I imagine it's something to do with Lit, of course. Or perhaps his family history.

But even though those are the most logical answers, my mind keeps dredging up the fluttery, phantom electricity I feel when I touch him, almost like he's one of my fated but not quite. It's an echo, a whisper of connection, no more. Nothing like the clear, primal feelings I have with Jared, Milo, and Landon.

However, it's something more than I've felt with anyone else since I arrived here. Perhaps it's just to do with our history. The connection I already had with him made more physical in this new, magical world.

It could be completely innocent.

But the small, dark corner of my brain that won't shut up keeps suggesting there's something more. My mind drifts back to being shut in his tiny little office, the air close with the scent of him, faint energy on the air. I was angry to find out he lied to me, but there's no denying the air had a charge, a tension, that coiled in my belly. That piece of my brain that likes to cause me trouble has twisted the memory, imagining him pulling me onto his desk, standing between my thighs and kissing me with a force that devours me whole.

So, safe to say my teenage crush is back full force, now aided by the fact that he's about a hundred times hotter, in his professor getup with sandy blonde curls, than he ever was as a ragged street kid with a buzz cut.

And I'm no longer a little girl in need of protection.

I make it through my classes with my brain in total la-la-land, clenching my thighs together whenever too visceral of a daydream strikes me. That I wore one of my short dresses with high boots today is completely unrelated to seeing Derrek later.

Thank god the guys take decent notes because I have not heard one word from my professors all day.

"…, Layla?"

We're at lunch and I've been completely tuned out, rolling my food around in my mouth and imagining its Derrek's tongue instead. *What the hell is wrong with me?* I nearly choke on the bite I'm chewing when I realize Landon said my name, but I don't know what he's asking.

I swallow and take a long sip of my water before I give him a sheepish smile. "Sorry, what did you say?"

The guys exchange a look. "I asked if you were ready for our bio exam or if you wanted to study this weekend," Landon replies slowly. "Are you alright, Layla? You've been kind of spacey all day."

Heat floods my cheeks. "Yeah, sorry I…" I don't have a good excuse. My mind is a complete blank aside from my 'hot for teacher' daydreams, and I'm certainly not about to tell those to the guys. "Derrek wants to talk to me before class, about... what we talked about before." I glance meaningfully down the table both ways, hoping they get the hint that I don't want to hash everything out in front of an audience. "So I've been thinking about what it could be."

"No problem, gorgeous," Jared leans back in his seat. "We can head to his office before class."

Panic rises in my chest, but I try to act cool. "No, if you don't mind, I want to talk to him alone first. I'll tell you guys the details later. You know, just in case I'm wrong and it's about how I'm failing Lit or something," I give a half-hearted laugh to play it off, but the three of them still look slightly suspicious.

Once again, it's Milo who saves the day. "Sure thing, Lex. You're entitled to your privacy like everyone else. But we're just a text away if you need us." He crumples up his napkin and tosses it on his empty tray, then stands and presses a warm kiss to my temple. "I'll see you after class, beautiful." His warm cedar scent envelopes me for just a second, the tingles from his kiss coursing through my body as he walks away.

Landon follows suit, also bidding me farewell with a spine-tingling kiss that threatens to turn me into a puddle despite the crowded cafeteria.

Jared waits for me to finish eating, insisting he's going to walk me to the English building and then sit in the lecture hall to read until class starts. After deepening our connection yesterday and heightening it with kissing, I realize the electric tingles I feel from Jared have altered. Now it's more like the thrumming reverberations of a guitar string, a vibration that starts at the point of contact and shoots straight to my core.

We cross the sunny quad holding hands, and suddenly the words tumble out of me.

"Jared, do you feel something when you touch me?"

"Feel something? Of course I do. I'm not a monster," he teases, affecting an exaggerated reaction of shock at my audacity.

I elbow him in the ribs. "You know what I mean. Whenever I touch you, or Milo or Landon, I feel like… electricity, but nice. Not an electric shock, but sort of pleasant, tingly sensations."

Jared's eyes drop to our clasped hands, and he considers for a moment as we walk. As if conducting an experiment, he lifts them and drags a fingertip from his free hand along my trapped knuckles. Tingles with that same reverberation course over my skin and my belly clenches.

"No," he concludes finally. "I always feel a little… I dunno, kind of spark in the air when I'm around you. Perhaps that's a little tingly? But when I touch you, I just feel your skin, nothing else."

"I see. Good to know." It seems this feeling is one-sided.

"What is it like? Is it the same with all three of us?"

"Actually, it was the same, until… yesterday," I admit, my cheeks heating. "At first it was just like a little tingle, a little shiver that ran over my skin whenever I touched one of you. I dunno if it was just the kissing, or how I feel closer to you now—since you let me in a little." I nudge him with my shoulder. "But now with you, it's different. But the same with the other two."

"Different how?"

I can tell he's excited that we suddenly have something I don't share with the other two.

"Um, instead of light tingles, it feels more like… a vibration. You know, like a guitar string?"

"Huh. Well, I don't have it, but it sounds cool. Maybe it's another alpha thing?"

"Yeah, that's what I was assuming. I just thought that because you guys were my fated, you might feel it, too."

"We felt the second you crossed into pack territory, and we can feel when you're nearby, or when your emotions change suddenly. It's kind of a vague feeling, at least for me. Landon talks about it more, but he's just really good at reading your facial expressions."

We've walked down the long cramped hallway of closed office doors, and finally reached Derrek's.

"Well, this is where I leave you, gorgeous." Jared wraps me in his muscular arms and flicks back the brim of his cap so he can kiss me properly.

I melt slightly, the vibration tied to a tightening coil in my belly, before I pull away. "Okay, get to class. I'll see you soon."

He winks, and when he turns to walk away, I swat him playfully on that fine, muscular butt he can't even hide in baggy jeans. Jared just looks over his shoulder and gives me a smirk, wagging his finger as if to discipline me while he walks away.

"If you're done playing grab-ass in the hallway, come in and close the door, Layla."

Derrek's voice is harsh and cold, and makes me jump before I scuttle to follow his instructions. Something about it is so professorial and commanding it makes my knees tremble.

I don't meet his gaze when I first enter, focusing instead on closing the door and setting down my backpack while I take my seat. But when I do, I'm not prepared for the anger that greets me. Derrek's green eyes are like cold stones in his handsome face, his expression furious. Instead of his typically disarming, laid-back posture, he stands at his full height, arms crossed over his chest.

If I thought he was hot before, this sudden turn to 'disappointed professor' takes it up a notch.

Heat floods my chest and I cross my legs tightly, tugging on the hem of my dress where a good deal of my thigh is exposed. Tension crackles in the air between us, although I'm still not sure why.

"You wanted to see me?" I ask hesitantly. He doesn't seem inclined to break the silence, but he's the one who told me to come.

"Yes. I asked you to come because we have important things to *discuss*. I didn't invite you to make out with your boyfriend in front of my office."

That pulls me up short. "It wasn't making out, Derrek. That was one kiss."

"Well, this is my place of work, and not the back row of a movie theater, so I'd appreciate it if you kept your teenage hormones caged for more appropriate locations."

I snort. "Oh please, this place is full of fated couples. They make out all over campus. That could hardly be the worst thing you've seen *today*, let alone in the week you've been here." Truthfully, my classmates are all over each other, often. I don't know how similar it is to a regular college, but the 'fated mates' thing really seems to give people a pass here.

Derrek continues to glare at me, the vein in his neck throbbing and his face tinged red.

It takes me a few seconds, but I finally put two and two together.

"This isn't just about kissing; this is about *me*, isn't it?" Indignation rises in my chest, setting fire to my blood. "I have just as much right to a little PDA as any other student here, and there are no rules about where that can and can't happen. I'll do you the favor of not making out on your desk, but other than that, you don't own this school and you don't own me, Derrek. I know you always acted like a big brother in LA, but I'm not your kid sister to boss around."

"It's not that," he retorts. "I just don't want to see it. This is my office. I should have a place where I don't have to."

"So close the door if you don't want to see what goes on in the hallway," I sneer.

"The door is closed!" He roars.

"So, what are you *complaining* about?" Our voices keep rising, and I know it's probably carrying to the neighboring offices, but I'm too pissed to care.

"Dammit Lex!" He shouts at me.

I stand abruptly, pushing back my chair. "You know what? Whatever you had to say doesn't fucking matter. I'm not going to sit here and take this shit. You have no right to act like you own the building, *or* me. Call me when you figure that out." With a huff, I yank my backpack from the ground and turn to the door, intending to sweep dramatically from his office. *Asshole*. And here I'd been fantasizing about this moment all day like a besotted school girl.

Just as I reach for the handle, his palms slam on the door above me, preventing me from opening it. The heat from his body surrounds me, and a tiny, frightened lump forms in my throat. I feel him press against the backs of my exposed thighs.

"Wait," he growls in a low, dangerous voice.

Hands trembling, I school my features to cold fury and turn slowly to face him. He's got nearly a foot of height on me, and I'm caged against the door with no way out short of kicking him in the balls.

I'm seriously considering it.

"What. Do. You. Want." I spit each word out slowly, deliberately. I'm the alpha, and he's seconds away from finding out what that truly means.

My gaze is locked on his, and I stare directly at his narrowed green eyes. He's standing so still I can hear his heart pounding in his chest, even over the low, heaving breaths he's drawing.

The moment drags out, and I refuse to back down. I can't issue him an alpha command, and my dominance means nothing to him. But even in the human world, I'd refuse to blink first. I'm not giving him a damn inch.

I expect him to sigh, to back away, throw his hands up and tell me to leave, maybe send me an apologetic text later.

Instead, he pushes in and kisses me roughly, claiming my body in one swift, feral move.

A gasp of surprise escapes my lips, and he takes advantage to plumb the depths of my mouth.

My brain switches off as my body switches on, pressing itself to him, my hands reaching up to pull on his shaggy curls.

Derrek moans, then buries his hand in my thick hair, clenching a fistful and tugging lightly. It sends hot rivers of lust down my spine, straight to my core, which is almost painful with need at this point. A desperate, whining sound escapes my lips.

He keeps the grip on my hair and rips his mouth from mine, chuckling darkly. "Mm, somehow I knew you'd like that," he murmurs, kissing along my jaw and nipping down my neck with his teeth. He pulls just a little more, exposing more neck for his wandering mouth and igniting a fresh course of sensation along my scalp. His free hand glides up the side of my thigh, first squeezing my butt before trailing between us. Excitement ripples across my stomach as his fingers drag over the sensitive skin, then proceed lower, cupping me firmly between my thighs, pushing gently on the damp fabric of my panties. A feral growl rumbles in his chest when my hips move, pressing against his hand.

My hands drop from his head, traveling along his body and tugging at the dress shirt tucked into his pants. I take seconds to get my fingers under the hem, and I press my hands to the hot, rock-hard flesh of his stomach, feeling the muscles flex. He drags his lips up along my jaw and reclaims my mouth roughly. I bend under him, giving in to his demanding pressure like water gives to the steel bow of a ship.

Everything about this moment is hot and intense. I can barely string two words together into a thought before some fresh sensation sends them shattering apart. *Kissing Derrek is nothing like kissing my fated.*

As if I've suddenly found a backbone, I straighten and press firmly against Derrek's chest, forcing his mouth away from mine. His fingers loosen, releasing my hair and body, and we stand, gasping as we stare at each other yet again. Except this time, it's a completely different tension.

"Lex," his tone is anguished, contrite, almost pleading. "I'm sorry, I shouldn't-"

"I have fated," I cut him off, panting. I don't want to hear his apologies, and I don't want to listen to him tell me it was a mistake. I already know.

It doesn't change the fact that I wanted it to happen, desperately. That it's taking every ounce of my willpower to keep my distance.

"Right, you have fated mates." His tone turns flat, and he leans against the chair I so recently vacated. "Regardless, I'm your professor, and it's completely improper for me to take advantage of you like that."

I snort. "Come off it, Derrek. Things may have changed since our days on the street, but not that much. You know me, and you know I don't give a lick about those sorts of rules. I do care about my fated, and how they'd feel. That's all."

He runs a hand through his tousled curls. "Right." Drawing in a deep breath, he stands, tucking his dress shirt back into his pants and straightening his belt buckle. Checking his watch, he adds, "Well, we're running out of time before class, so do you still want to hear what I invited you here for, or should we table it?"

I tug the hem of my dress. "I'm here, let's talk."

Nodding, Derrek passes behind his desk and takes a seat, adjusting his pants. It has been a heroic effort for me not to ogle the outline of the erection I felt against my stomach while he lounged in full view. I sigh with relief when we're both settled into our chair and I can't see it any more.

"I wanted to talk to you, because I think I may know someone who can answer your questions about the curse. If there's anyone who can find a way out of it, it's her."

I was just starting to cool down, but this exciting bit

of news has my heart rate climbing again. "Who is it? Someone in the pack?"

"Not exactly," he hedges. "I found out that my grannie is still alive, and she's old. Like, way beyond the realm of *normal* old. It probably has something to do with her being a witch. She doesn't live on Montrose Pack lands, hasn't for decades. We used to go visit her once in a while, but she likes to keep her distance from 'the noise of the magical world,' as she put it. As soon as my mom took over pack duties, she retired."

"How much could she really know about it? She's a generation removed, isn't she? My great grandma was only fifteen when they cursed us."

"Lex, I'm telling you, she's old. She was there—she remembers it."

Chapter Eighteen

MILO

~

I have to admit, when Lex sends a group text telling us she and Jared are playing hooky and the prof is giving them a pass, I'm concerned. Landon and I exchange a worried glance, then pack our stuff up and hustle out of the library. We meet at Landon's Grand Cherokee in the student lot and waited for the explanation.

Jared throws his hands up as soon as he sees our faces. "Hey, don't look at me. This is something to do with Professor Smoothie-pants- ow!" Lex punched him in the arm. "Fine, *Derrek*, and what he told Layla before class. She hasn't clued me in yet, said she wanted to tell us all together."

Lex's cheeks are bright with color, her eyes practically glowing with excitement. "You guys will not *believe* it. It turns out that Derrek's grandma is like, freaking ancient, and she was alive when the curse was made. It was her mom who did it. She was *there*. He said he can take me to her place so I can ask her how to undo it."

"No way in hell." Jared crosses his arms. "That sounds like a terrible idea."

"I'm afraid I have to agree with Jared," Landon adds in a gentler tone. "It's too dangerous to go to Pack Montrose. You know what happened to your great aunt."

Lex's tone sharpens. "In case you all have forgotten, I'm the alpha here, not you. And his grandma isn't on Montrose lands. Apparently she tries to avoid being around magic users as much as possible. He remembers where she lives because he used to visit occasionally with his mom." Mimicking Jared's posture, she crosses her arms over her chest and stands her ground, glaring around and daring us to argue.

I'm almost certain there's more she's holding back, so I bite my tongue and wait.

"I dunno, Layla." Jared shakes his head. "It still sounds like a bad idea."

"Well, that's too fucking bad, because I'm going. And I want you all to come with me."

"Wait, you do?" Landon's voice is positively hopeful now.

"Yeah, I do. I would have told you that sooner if you hadn't been in a rush to tell me what a bad idea it is." The sarcastic curl of her lip draws a chuckle from me.

I push off the side of the car. "Yeah, I'd say you guys earned that one. But I'm in, Lex. I go where you go —always."

The beaming smile she gives me in response makes my heart flutter in my chest, and I smile back at her.

"Tomorrow afternoon," she states confidently. "It's over an hour's drive from here. Derrek doesn't have any afternoon classes, and neither do Landon and I. You two," she gestures to me and Jared, "will have to play hooky for the afternoon. And Jared, you're probably going to skip practice again. I apologize in advance if the coach punishes you for it. Of course you don't have to go…"

"No, I'll be there. Someone's gotta have your back besides these two bean-poles," he snorts.

"Okay, great! This is it, guys. I feel it." She's genuinely excited, and everything in me is excited with her.

I want Lex to be happy, and if that means going off on this crazy quest to track down an old lady who likely won't know a single useful bit of information, then that is what we'll do.

Even if I agree that it's a terrible idea.

Jared

Landon drives Lex home. Ordinarily, Milo would go with them, but he insists he's behind on his studying and is going to use the extra time to catch up, so he heads back to the library and waits for me after practice.

Guilt swims in my chest, knowing the team is counting on me and I'm going to no-show again tomorrow. I push myself harder than normal during practice. It's become so routine I don't even have to think about the physical work anymore, let alone the plays. Coach announces them, and muscle memory sends me off in the right direction every time.

I'm bigger, faster, or stronger than about 90% of the team. Even as a freshman, and even though I'm shorter than half of them. So I work hard, and I set the example at practice after practice, putting guys three years my senior to shame as they fall out, panting, during a run.

The result is that Coach is pleased, but I'm exhausted when I finally meet Milo at my truck.

And I *still* have to study.

"We're getting Badger's," I warn him as we clamber in. I'm starving. My stomach feels like it's eating me from the inside out.

Milo doesn't say anything—he knows how I get when I'm hungry.

So it isn't until we've devoured enough burgers and fries to feed a normal family of four that he speaks.

"Jared, how are you feeling about this little field trip tomorrow?"

I turn to him sharply. "Bad. I don't like it. But she's the alpha, and she doesn't want to keep hearing what *we* think she shouldn't do. I want to support her, so I don't really see any option but to go, and hope it doesn't blow up in our faces."

"Agreed." He nods, thoughtfully sipping from his shake. "But no one says we have to go *alone.*"

"We're not going alone. With Landon and Layla, not to mention Professor What's-his-name-"

"His name is Professor Westin," Milo interrupts mildly.

"I know his name," I snap. "I just don't like the guy. I don't like the way he looks at Layla."

"This is old news. We all know how you feel about him. You were saying?"

"That's five of us, hardly alone. Definitely enough for one old lady."

"But what if it's not just one old lady? And what if Derrek isn't on our side? Then it's four against two."

My body tenses. "Wait, you think he might be setting us up? Dude, why didn't you say something?"

"I know nothing for sure, but I'm trying to avoid alienating Lex any further. I think it's the smart move to have some backup, that's all. In case it's not everything that Lex is hoping for."

I narrow my eyes, thinking, as I finish up my last few fries.

"You're right. It's probably smart to have some backup. So, what do you have in mind?"

Chapter Nineteen

LAYLA

~

After our morning classes, we gather in the parking lot and take Landon's SUV.

To say that the atmosphere is tense would be an understatement.

The weather is pretty enough outside; although there are some threatening clouds on the horizon, it's mostly blue sky and sunny, with crisp fall breezes rustling the leaves as we drive by.

However, I probably should have expected that despite the roomy interior, the ride would be anything but comfortable, given my companions.

Derrek took the front passenger seat to give Landon directions. Even though I know he's technically almost a decade older than us, I still can't quite wrap my head around it. It seems strange, however, to have our Lit professor riding in a packed vehicle we're typically in for coffee runs and scarfing french fries.

I'm in the middle of the back seat with Jared and Milo flanking my sides, and there's a weird tension in the car I can't quite dispel. My valiant efforts to engage the guys in different conversations continue to be met with short, clipped answers.

Landon and Derrek seem to do alright up front; the latter providing turn-by-turn directions and engaging Landon in light conversation about the weather and the area. Landon seems pretty chill, although his knuckles do whiten on the steering wheel from time to time.

I'm using the ride to test my alpha skills of sensing the emotional climate of the pack. As we drive through town, I can sense the general contentment with the occasional flare of anger or frustration. I still have no way of identifying the individuals who aren't happy, but part of me wonders if that will change when I am 'officially' alpha, or it's just like an early warning signal. A useful tool to know someone is unhappy, but not an exact science.

Once we leave town, I lose a sense of the individuals, and eventually the feeling fades altogether when we leave pack lands.

I realize with a start that I haven't been out of Smoky Falls since I arrived. Instinctively, I glance at my phone, setting a mental timer that no matter what happens, I have to be back within 24 hours.

But even though we're off pack land, I can still

sample the emotions of my fated. Landon is a little nervous, which is definitely understandable. Milo is calmly tapping on his phone and appears perfectly serene, but there's a sharp edge of tension to his emotions. Sort of like he's calm, but extremely alert.

Of course, I can't really sense Derrek's emotions the same way, but Jared is impossible to misread—everything about his posture screams tense. His leg won't stop twitching; his gaze is permanently fixed on the back of Derrek's head rest as if he's attempting to develop laser vision and burn his way through, and even his hands fidget in his lap, picking at his cuticles.

He feels exactly what he's showing me. I reach over and claim one hand, threading my fingers through his before he makes himself bleed.

His eyes dart to mine and I smile encouragingly. His answering smile is tight, but he draws in a deep breath. "Sorry gorgeous, I'm just worried."

"I know." I squeeze his hand. "But we *have* to do this. If there's a chance we can stop the curse, wouldn't that be worth it?"

"Depends on what 'it' is," he replies in a low voice. "We really don't know what we're walking into. You getting hurt is definitely not worth it, in my book."

"I won't," I promise, knowing full well I have no way to keep it.

Jared gives me another half-hearted smile, but I know he doesn't really mean it. He's just trying to comfort me.

"Just relax, man," Milo pipes up from my other side.

"It won't do you any good to spend the entire ride tweaking out. Save it for when it counts."

He looks meaningfully at Jared, who nods, swallows, and goes back to staring at Derrek's head rest.

An uneasy feeling swirls in my stomach. I hope they don't have anything planned that would hurt Derrek. They certainly have no reason to hate him.

Liar, my dark little voice whispers. *They have every reason to hate him. To hate you for what you did.*

My palms start to sweat and I disengage from Jared's hand gently, wiping mine on my pant legs.

Guilt is a funny thing. It shows up suddenly, making my stomach flip-flop and bringing bile to my throat at the most inopportune times. Then it disappears for long stretches, only to rear its ugly head once more when I least expect it.

I was able to shove it down in the wake of Derrek's proposal yesterday, and I enjoyed the ride alone with Landon, talking about his music without restraint or fear of being overheard.

It wasn't until he walked me up to the door and leaned in to kiss me goodbye that I panicked. Guilt flooded my system, wondering if I would taste or smell like Derrek, if he would *know* I'd been all over the older man an hour earlier. I gave him a hug and a quick peck on the lips, then darted inside.

It's strange, being of two minds about it. One part of me relives the entire exchange repeatedly, luxuriating in every delicious moment of tension between us, every rough touch of his hands, every feeling under my fingertips.

And the other part of me swims in a sea of guilt, imagining how my fated would feel if they knew, if they had seen. The tension between all four of them is already thick enough to cut with a knife—what would happen if they knew he'd kissed me? Milo and Landon said Jared is super protective, and even though Derrek has filled out in the last year, he's nowhere near Jared's size when it comes to muscle. Plus, Jared has that wolf shifter strength and healing, and Derrek apparently has none of it.

Worrying about what they would do is enough to drive me insane. I don't want to hurt them. Our feelings for each other grow deeper by the day and I know the connection we share is special—it has been from the first moment I met each of them.

But I can't deny my past, either. And like it or not, Derrek was there for me when no one else was. He protected me, looked after me, and never so much as laid a hand on me, even though I would have been an easy target. I'm an adult, and even though he's ten years my senior, he's not a predator. Despite everything, he's trying to help me escape this curse that doesn't affect him at all.

It's as if the connection we had for all those years has thickened, boiling down to something sweeter, more meaningful, that continues to pull us together. I can't deny what I feel for him any more than I can deny my connection to my fated.

And I'm hopelessly caught in the middle. I try to keep looking forward instead of dwelling on the past. If I can break this curse, if I can get out from under the oppression of all the good and the bad that Smoky Falls has thrust upon me, perhaps the path forward will become clearer. Maybe if we're no longer cursed, I won't *need* fated mates, and our feelings and desires will change somehow. A painful dart shoots through me at the idea, as if just considering *not* having all three of my fated is enough to break me. Is it greedy to want them *all*?

Anxiety floods my body, and I'm filled with nervous energy. I need to get out, to get away. It's ironic that even here, off of pack lands, I'm surrounded by my fated, both literally and by the expectations they hold for me. There's no way I can just accept being cursed, being stuck in Smoky Falls for the rest of my life. This has to be the beginning of the end of this curse. *It has to be.*

My pant legs are damp from palm sweat when we turn off the paved road onto a narrow gravel drive. Trees encroach on all sides, and the sky overhead darkens as the clouds that were distant when we left close in.

An ominous sense of foreboding settles in my chest, making it difficult to draw in breath.

I finally admit to myself that this could be a bad idea. We're going to visit a witch, a very old and powerful one, according to Derrek, who was the daughter of the witch that cursed my family, my entire pack. None of us have any magic or skills to defend ourselves. We can't even shift at this hour, thanks to the curse.

A million reasons I'm a terrible leader and this is a bad idea flood my brain, on top of the worry that my fated might get hurt or my trust in Derrek might be misplaced.

No, I trust Derrek, I repeat to myself. If I know nothing else, it's that Derrek cares about me, and he's trying to help me.

The car slows to a stop, and Derrek tucks away his phone before turning around in his seat.

"Okay guys, we're here."

Chapter Twenty

MILO

~

I send one last text message before climbing out of the back seat and offering Lex my hand to get down. We've stopped at a dead end, where a small, old but clearly loved cottage rests, nestled in the trees.

A narrow front porch runs the length of the building, and a single rocking chair sits near the door. Loads of odd little ornaments decorate the front, wind chimes made from all sorts of natural things like snail shells, twigs, and small stones. Bushes that likely boast colorful blossoms in the spring, but now are little more than brown twigs, line the porch.

I hear nothing but wind rustling the leaves of the trees that seem to lean in protectively over the house. A chill licks up my spine, the feeling of being watched sending goosebumps running over my arms.

A quick glance at the others confirms everyone is just standing here, taking it all in.

I step up to Landon and whisper a quick suggestion, and he obligingly climbs back in the SUV, turning and parking it so it's off to the side of the small clearing and facing outward, back to the road.

In case we need to make a quick escape.

"So, now what?" Jared's voice is terse, and he glares at the professor, waiting for an answer.

"Well, I suppose I ought to go up and knock. I haven't seen her in a long time." Derrek's voice is soft, almost reverent, and tinged with nerves.

"Wait, she doesn't know we're coming?" Lex's tone is an octave higher than normal, betraying her emotions as clearly as she can read ours.

"I didn't exactly have a way to contact her," Derrek looks down at her upturned face with a fond smile and chuckles. "She doesn't have a phone. But don't worry, she'll remember me."

Movement to my left catches my attention as Jared steps closer to Lex, his arms crossed and the muscles in his jaw clenching.

I know what's bothering him, and I see it. There's something between Lex and the Lit professor; the way they gaze at each other is almost... intimate.

My own jaw clenches. *Whatever she needs*, I repeat silently to myself. If she needs this guy in her life, it's my duty to support her. We're still her fated, and he doesn't change that.

"Let's get this show on the road," Jared breaks the silence, drawing Derrek's gaze away from our mate. "I don't want to be standing out here when the storm hits."

And it's coming soon. Energy crackles in the air, even though the wind has died down. It's only a matter of time before the storm blast hits us, followed by a signature Smoky Mountain downpour.

"Right-o," Derrek says, then strides forward and climbs the porch, rapping lightly on the door. The rest of us remain in the clearing below.

After a moment, the door opens, and the fuzzy outline of an older woman appears through the screen door. She studies Derrek for a moment before speaking in a croaky, ancient voice. "Leaf? Is that you?"

My eyes dart to the others, who are all glancing at each other, confused. *Who the hell is Leaf?*

"Hi, Grannie," Derrek answers sheepishly.

"By the goddess, it *is* you! Come in, come in, bring your friends. It's about to be very wet outside."

Derrek turns and gestures for us to come forward, a delighted grin on his face. Lex takes the first step, and we fall in behind her. He holds the door open for us to pass through, and we end up in a small, cluttered but cozy living room, complete with a blazing fireplace. It's filled with earthy knickknacks; dried plants dangle from strings overhead, polished river stones, bowls of snail shells and particularly colorful leaves.

Speaking of…

"Leaf?" I mutter to Derrek.

"Yes, that's his name," the old lady's voice calls from her tiny kitchen. "His *true* name. My Anya named him that, because he trembled like a little leaf after he was born." She comes shuffling out and I finally get a good look at her. While she's a little stooped, she's still tall for a woman, easily a half foot taller than Lex. She's wearing a long wool dress, with a thick shawl wrapped over her shoulders and pinned with an enamel brooch shaped like a fox.

"I'm Leaf's Grannie. You are welcome to call me the same. Or Shuya, if you must. It's so nice to meet you all." Her voice may be a little shaky and the soft folds of her skin definitely speak of age, but there's nothing else that seems old about this woman. Her movements are sharp, almost bird-like, but more like a hawk than a dove. Glittering, clear eyes, dark blue like deep water, rove over each of us, and I feel stripped naked under her gaze. Something tells me she misses nothing.

"Grannie, this is Jared, Landon, and Milo," Derrek introduces us. "And this is-"

"Harridan." She cuts him off. "Not a doubt in my mind." Her sharp gaze travels over Lex, landing on her eyes and holding her gaze.

Lex does well. She lifts her chin and gazes back at the old woman patiently.

"Layla Harris," my mate corrects her.

"Bah, you're a Lilliana, through-and-though. What-ever you call yourself." Shuya steps forward, almost uncomfortably close to Lex, and I resist the urge to intervene. Lex doesn't move a muscle.

"Yep," the old woman mutters, seemingly to herself. "Definitely Lilliana. You're... something different, though, aren't you, girl? You don't taste the same as the others."

Something in my stomach clenches. Just the way she says *taste* makes me think of Hansel and Gretel, and the hairs rise on the back of my neck.

"Grannie can taste magic," Derrek rushes to explain as my brothers and I bristle. "It's how most witches operate."

"That's right," she agrees, stepping back and bustling into her kitchen again. "You're all from the old pack. I could taste it on the air before you even came inside." The high, keening whistle of a teakettle rises, then falls again almost immediately. "Sit!" The old lady barks. "I'm coming with the tea."

Derrek gestures us to a wide table made from rough planks and moves toward the kitchen.

"Sit down, Leaf. I don't need your help. I'm not dead yet," she chuckles drily.

We slide into the bench seats on either side, Jared beside Lex and Landon with me, leaving the end seats for Derrek and Shuya.

She busies herself pouring tea, distributing delicate, handmade clay cups to each of us, along with a plate of cookies that have tiny flowers baked onto the top.

"Grannie, I-"

"Oh, I know why you're here. Calm down," she

mutters, finally easing into the wooden chair. "We'll get to that. Just be a civil guest for a few minutes and enjoy your tea." She leans to the side, stage-whispering to Lex. "Always in a hurry, this one."

Lex grins and lifts her cup, sniffing the fragrant steam.

I examine my cup, more than a little dubious about the contents. Aside from Derrek, the others are all hesitating, blowing on the steam or sniffing it suspiciously.

"Oh, for goddess' sake, I'm not trying to poison you. It's just chamomile." The old lady lifts her mug and takes a long sip. "I grow it in my garden. It's good for soothing the nerves and you lot seem about to shake out of your skin."

The snort pushes from my nose, but I obediently sip the scalding-hot tea—it's definitely just chamomile—and reach for a cookie. It's some sort of shortbread and has a delicate purple sprig on the top.

After the buildup of excitement to get here, then being told to slow down and be polite guests, I'm left a little confused as to how we're supposed to proceed. Shuya seems quite content to enjoy her tea and cookies without speaking, and the rest of us follow suit. I can't help but wonder if she truly knows why we're here. Also, why she and Derrek aren't even speaking... from the sounds of it, she hasn't seen him in at least a decade... isn't she curious about what he's been up to? Or has he been here more recently than he let on?

Despite Lex's faith in the guy, I'm not willing to trust him any further than I can throw him.

Shuya, however, I like. She reminds me of my own grandma.

A loud rumble of thunder echoes through the house, followed by a deafening clap that shakes the walls.

Shuya cackles with delight. "Oh, it's a good one, no doubt about that! My pumpkins love a good drink before harvest." She settles back in her seat and smacks her lips just as the roar of heavy rain begins overhead. "Well, I suppose we ought to get down to business, Lilliana." Shuya turns her beady eyes to Lex.

"It's Layla," my mate tries to correct her, but the old lady slaps her hand on the table.

"No, no, no. Lilliana is your *true* name, just like my Leaf. You can't fully claim your power until you claim the name. It doesn't matter what you call yourself, but when dealing with those that are magically inclined, you weaken yourself by denying it, girl. There is nothing more powerful than your true name. Truth is powerful."

Layla's eyes flash, her voice strong and rising as she speaks. "The *truth* is I never heard that name until just over a year ago. I've been Layla my entire life. The *truth* is my family was cursed, and *that* name came with the weight of a magical feud that I knew nothing about, but now am singularly responsible, at eighteen, for protecting an entire pack from. The *truth* is-"

"The *truth* is that life is unfair, child," the old woman cuts her off gently. "That doesn't make it any less true."

"If I'd never left LA, I'd never have been cursed," Lex argues.

"No, you've been cursed since before you were born. The difference is, you simply didn't know it before, like you didn't know your true name." Shuya leans toward Lex, her eyes narrowing. "But now you do. So the question is, what are you going to do about it?"

"That's why I'm here," Lex throws up her hands. "Derrek thought you might know something that could help me."

The old woman's eyes flash to Derrek. "My Leaf is a smart boy," she seems to agree. "He left too, tried to forget his true name, but he's back now, isn't he?"

"So, do you know something that can help me or not?"

The woman's wizened face curves into a clever grin. "I know something that could help Lilliana Harridan. But it wouldn't be of much use to a Layla Harris, I'm afraid."

Lex realizes she's been outfoxed immediately, and her teeth dig deep into the flesh of her lower lip to restrain the retort that's clearly on the tip of her tongue.

The downpour on the roof is deafening in the silence as we all wait with bated breath. The pressure of the storm sets my teeth on edge, raising the hairs on the back of my neck again.

Lex pulls in a deep breath, takes a slow sip of tea, and tries again.

"My name is Lilliana Harridan. I was born Lilliana

Harridan, and I am the alpha of the Smoky Falls pack, who was apparently cursed by your mother. Do you know of a way I can undo the curse?"

Shuya mimics her movement, casually sipping her tea. "The truth is a tricky thing, dear. It may be something you don't want to hear."

"I promise you, I want to hear it. Please."

The old woman's eyes glaze over momentarily, as if she's mentally traveled to another place. When she returns her focus to the room, she's no longer serene or patient.

"There is danger headed this way, and you all must leave. Now!" She pushes away from the table and starts trying to shoo us from our seats.

The other guys and I jump to our feet at the mention of danger, but Lex refuses to budge. "First, tell me how to break the curse."

"There's no time for this, girl. I always love visitors, but you've overstayed your welcome. Go. Come visit another day. I'll make lemon bars."

Landon tries to tug her toward the door, but Lex doesn't move an inch.

She slams her fist on the table, and when she speaks, her voice is fused with the alpha double-timbre. Surely she knows it won't work on the witch, but I'm uncertain if she's even doing it on purpose at this point. Standing, she commands, "Tell me how to break the curse!"

The old woman snorts. "You can't order me around, girl, alpha or not. You hold no power here. And you know how to break the curse; you've known it all along. But none of you can see what is right in front of your nose. Until you do, there's nothing I can do for you.

"But I mean it when I say you have to leave, now. Azalea is coming, and I can't protect you from her. *You need to run.* You're nearly out of time."

"Lex!" Derrek's voice is strained, and when I glance his way, his face has gone deathly pale. "She's not kidding. We need to leave."

"Wait, who is Azalea?" Thrown off, Lex allows Landon to tug her a few steps. Jared looks as if he's considering throwing her over his shoulder and bulldozing his way outside, and I'm about ready to encourage him.

The tension in the air that I took for excess energy from the storm has thickened, growing to a painful crackling along my skin like electric shocks. Whoever this Azalea person is, she's bad news. My phone buzzes angrily in my pocket; I don't need to take it out. I know it's my early warning system.

"Lex," I growl, panic giving way to the crawling sensation under my skin. "We have to go! We'll come back another time. I will come *whenever* you want, I promise."

Her green eyes are conflicted, looking around at all of us. "But we didn't get the answers we need! I don't understand-"

The loud rumble of an engine outside cuts her off.

It's already too late to escape. Whoever this Azalea person is, she's here.

Chapter Twenty-One

LAYLA

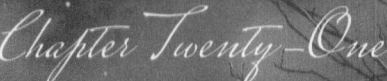

The growing sense of dread fills my stomach with snakes. I've fought my every instinct to get the answers we came for, but I know it's too late when I hear the deep, thrumming purr of a loud engine outside.

The rain has slowed from a downpour to a light pattering against the roof, and we can hear the engine cut off and car door slam in exquisite detail.

My fated gather around me, forming a semicircle between me and the door. Derrek joins them, stepping out in front of us all, blocking my view of the door. I step to the side to see better—I always like to know what's coming at me.

Shuya sighs heavily, sitting back in her chair and taking another sip of tea.

The arrival doesn't bother knocking. First the screen door squeaks loudly, then the heavy wooden door pushes inside, revealing a tall, slender, cloaked figure in all black. It almost looks like a costume—who wears a long wool cape with a hood so deep you can't see their face?—but she quickly pushes it back on her head.

She has power; I feel it prickling over my skin. But my first thought is—*she looks like a movie star.*

The young woman strides into the house slowly, water from her high-heeled boots pooling on the wooden floor. Her pale, oval face is flawless, with a pretty flush on her cheeks to set off full, blood-red lips, and eyes like the deep blue ocean sparkle with amusement. Her lips curl into a delighted smile, and she reaches back to fluff silky blonde hair.

Her gaze never leaves Derrek.

"Well, isn't this a delightful surprise, cousin," her grin widens. "It's been too long, Leaf." Azalea's voice is sweet and seductive, with a smoky edge.

Every muscle in Derrek's back is tense. "Azalea," he grinds out from between clenched teeth. "Fancy seeing you here. *Unannounced.*"

"I could say the same thing, cousin. We didn't know you were back in town, or we'd have thrown you a little welcome party. It's a lucky thing my charms let me know when Grannie has visitors. Hey, Grannie," she leans around Derrek and wiggles her fingers. "And... Leaf, aren't you going to introduce me to your friends?"

The witch saunters closer and I feel the clawing, tugging under my skin, my wolf begging to be set free.

She pulls in a deep breath, then her features twist as if she smells something bad. "Oh dear, I'm afraid you've made friends with kids from the wrong side of the tracks, cousin. Tsk, tsk," she wags a finger at him with another vicious smile. "What would the alpha say?"

"*I'm* the alpha, and I say Derrek is free to do what he wants," I snarl. Witch or not, I can't take the deference he's giving her. He's practically frozen in place, whether from fear or something else, I can't tell.

Her expression widens in false surprise, and she ambles closer to the dining table. "Oh, she's feisty, the new Harridan. Not very smart though, is she?"

"You leave her alone, Az," Derrek growls.

"Azalea, you know the rules, no magic in my house!" Shuya's voice, while creaky, is laced with power.

The witch places a hand on Shuya's shoulder. "I know, Grannie. I just came to check on you, make sure you're okay. I hate that you're out here all by yourself with no one to protect you. You never know when *rogues* will show up," her voice turns from sweetly condescending to a snarl, complete with a feral glance in Derrek's direction. Instantly, she reverts to sugary sweet. "I wish you'd move closer to the pack so we could look out for you."

"I'm quite happy where I'm at, Azalea," the older woman answers stiffly. "Leaf, you and your friends ought to be going now."

"Yes, run along and play with your little friends," Azalea sneers. "Grannie and I need to have a chat."

The guys close ranks around me as Azalea claims my seat at the table. We walk toward the door, and I don't dare look back until the screen door slams behind us.

"Keep going," Derek mutters under his breath.

The rain has almost completely cleared by now, but the gravel clearing is more of a lake than a driveway at this point. We pick our way between the puddles toward Landon's SUV, and I pull in a deep sigh of relief, the tension uncoiling.

Just then, the crunch of gravel draws our attention to a new vehicle arriving, and the guys once again cluster around me.

To my absolute shock, Amber and several members of the football team, including the Westley twins, pile out of a large black SUV.

Amber runs up to hug me, and the guys step away. "You guys okay? We saw that car come in and let Milo know, but we figured when we didn't hear back, we should just come check it out and see if you needed help."

"You guys followed us all the way here to help me?" Warmth pools in my chest, spreading outward.

Amber grins. "Of course, you're our alpha, and besides, we're friends, right?" The guys all grunt and mumble in agreement.

My eyes dart to Milo. "You did this?"

He shrugs. "It seemed prudent to have a backup plan."

"Well thanks," I tell him. "And thank you guys for being here. But I think we ought to go. Just follow us back to the main road-"

"Hey Leaf!" Azalea's shout sends a trickle of icy dread down my spine, and as one we turn to face her.

She strides in our direction, hands innocently at her sides, smiling coyly.

"What do you want, Azalea? We're leaving."

"I just wanted to return something of yours." The static feeling of her magic crackles over my skin, and my wolf starts clawing to escape again.

Derrek waves a hand, encouraging us to get back in the cars. "Whatever it is, I'm sure I don't want it." He turns and places a palm on my shoulder, guiding me to the vehicle.

It happens in a split second: a sharp crack of power echoes through the clearing, followed by feet crunching on gravel, then a wet smacking noise. By the time I'm able to turn back around, Azalea is grinning evilly, her arm outstretched in my direction. A heavy thud sounds at my feet, and I look down to see one of the Westley twins on the ground, a dark red stain spreading across his white t-shirt, and a silver knife handle sticking out of his back. A blood-curdling shriek rips from Amber's chest, and she dives to his side. The wail coming from her can only mean one thing: it's Jeremy, her fated.

Azalea cackles. "Well, I certainly didn't see that

coming! But pack loyalty has always come with a heavy price, hasn't it? Anyway, there's your knife back, Leaf. I thought you should know, if you decide to grow a pair and finish the job, the pack would welcome you back. Tata!"

She turns and strides back into the house.

Dropping to my knees, I try to stop Amber from pulling the knife out of his chest. "No, Amber, we have to leave it in, it'll just make him bleed out faster." One of the boys from her car pulls her arms back, keeping her away from the handle. She screams and struggles, but he's got a hold of her. I'm no doctor, but even I can tell my advice is basically useless. The blood has poured from him in a river, mixing with the rainwater and turning the ground puddles a dark, rusty red. And he's not moving.

"Keep an eye on the house," Derrek commands. "Let me know if she sticks one toe back outside."

He crouches down beside me and tips Jeremy's body up, only to confirm what I feared: the knife has gone completely through to the other side.

"Lex, there's nothing we can do," he says softly. "Even if it were a normal wound, we wouldn't be able to save him. It's gone straight through his heart... he's already gone."

"What do you mean, a normal wound?" I ask, shock making me hyper-fixate on details. It's just too much to process.

"It's a spelled blade. It would take enormous

amounts of magic to heal any wound made by it, let alone one that's instantly fatal."

"How do you know that? It could just be a normal knife, right?"

"I'm sorry Lex, but I know. I recognize it—it's mine."

My heart sinks, and my body starts to tremble. "No," I say, softly, under my breath. "No!" I reach out with my senses, but aside from the grief and fury from the pack members standing around me, I can't sense anything from Jeremy. It's as if she snuffed his light out like a candle. It's just... *gone*. I can't connect to him anymore.

Fury builds under my skin, hot and bubbling, replacing the sick, trembling feeling with something powerful and hard as steel.

I stand, glaring at the house. At the witch who just casually tossed a knife at my back and murdered one of my pack.

I get one step away before the vice-like grip of three sets of hands is upon me.

"Let me go," I snarl. "I have to avenge my pack!"

"Lex, you can't! This isn't the place. You can't shift right now, and she'll kill you." Milo makes sense, but at this moment, I refuse to listen to reason.

"I can't let her get away with it," I growl, the sound rumbling in my chest.

"You will make her pay when the time is right." Landon's voice is gentle, but I won't be soothed.

"Release me," I snarl, using the alpha command to force them to comply. They have no power to hold me.

As one, my mates release my arms, and I get one more step forward before I'm hit in the face with a blast of air. It shocks me momentarily, setting me back on my heels.

Derrek wastes no time, scooping me up and climbing into the back seat, keeping me tightly in his lap. "Hurry, we have to go!"

Landon and Milo jump in the front and Jared joins us in the back, pulling the door closed as we peel out. The other group has already pulled Jeremy's body into their vehicle and is right behind us.

Coming back to my senses, I snarl, thrashing at the arms pinning me tightly to Derrek's body. "Let me go!" My alpha command echoes through my head, but Derrek isn't affected.

"I can't do that Lex. I'm sorry, I don't want to see you get hurt."

"Landon-" I start with the alpha voice rumbling in my chest, but Derrek claps a hand over my mouth.

"If you order him to stop, he will, and put all of us in danger. *Is that what you want?* Or do you want to do your job as alpha and protect your pack?"

A frustrated, animalistic scream pours from my throat. He's right, and I have no choice. We've already lost someone, and we've got no weapons against a powerful witch.

Finally giving in, I sag against Derrek's chest.

"If I let you go, will you be smart and make the right decision to keep everyone safe?" He asks carefully.

I nod, and his arms loosen, allowing me to slide to the seat between him and Jared.

Slumped over, I rest my head in my hands and do my very best not to cry.

I can't believe how utterly and completely I've fucked up.

Chapter Twenty-Two

LAYLA

~

After riding in a state I can only describe as numb for an indeterminate amount of time, I suddenly come back to life with the realization that, as alpha, I probably have a lot of important things to do regarding Jeremy's passing.

I send a message to Roxanne, confessing where we went and the summary of what happened. She can judge all she wants from afar. But I'm the alpha and I make the decisions, and the pack lives with it.

Or dies with it.

Roxanne gives me instructions on where to go, and I relay them to Landon. Milo sends them to his friends in the other vehicle. Once we arrive in town, I'll have to accept the responsibility for a death that was easily preventable. If we'd never left the pack grounds, it never would have happened.

Those boys weren't even meant to be there.

But they came to protect you, their alpha, I argue with myself. *If you hadn't gone, they wouldn't have gone.*

No one asked them!

Your fated did.

The guilt and accusations float around and around in my head, coiling in useless circles.

Eventually, I start reflecting on the trip, every individual little moment, trying to assess what I could have done differently.

Obviously, not going at all would be a great place to start. She didn't even tell me the one thing I went there to ask. Her voice echoes in my head. *"… you know how to break the curse; you've known it all along. But none of you can see what is right in front of your nose. Until you do, there's nothing I can do for you."*

What does that even mean? I don't know anything about breaking the curse, or I wouldn't have been there asking.

All that time wasted, sipping tea and talking about true names, just to finish with nothing.

And I should have left when she told us to. I'm the reason we didn't get out on time.

And I hesitated outside, too. We were free to go, could have been already on the road before Azalea came back out.

I never should have turned my back on her. If I hadn't, she wouldn't have had a target to toss that knife. Jeremy wouldn't have had to jump in front of me to save my life.

So many things I did wrong. So much responsibility to bear.

My mind goes over every word, every moment, as the silent ride continues.

There *has* to be something to her statement that I already know how the break the curse. She didn't just say I was blind to it; she said we *all* were.

At some point, we'll have to sit down together and try to puzzle it out, but for now, I'm too tired for riddles.

Speaking of, where did Azalea come from? She called Derrek her cousin, which means they're related through his mom. But he never mentioned a cousin when he told me the pack expected him to be their new witch. He sort of made it sound like he and his mom were on their own.

But clearly not, since there was evidently a cousin around.

My mind draws up every word she said, pulling them apart for clues.

And then, as if I'm putting together a puzzle for which I've never seen the entire picture, the full story clicks into place in my mind.

Finally—*finally*—it all makes sense. Every part fits. How Derrek found me, Azalea's taunting words, the silver knife... I've been completely, utterly blind.

Fighting the urge to clamber into Jared's lap, I lean casually against him instead. He wraps a warm, muscular arm around my shoulders, and I shift over so no part of my body is touching Derrek's. The thrumming vibration of our bond soothes me, and I shoot another text message to Roxanne.

When we get back, we'll handle Jeremy and his family first.

And then we'll deal with Derrek.

~

Landon

~

I can feel the emotions coming off Layla, and it's a heavy jumble. Pain, guilt, sadness, fear, betrayal, and a white-hot ribbon of fury. As the driver I can't do much for her from here, but I sure as shit am not letting her go home alone tonight. I'd be willing to bet none of us are.

The tightness of my shoulders doesn't ease until we get back on pack lands, and I drive us straight to the town security office, where Roxanne is waiting with the officers.

If it had been the death of a normie on pack lands, they would bring in the county sheriff and create a whole police report.

But given the circumstances, things are a bit different.

We pull into the parking lot just as a sleek silver BMW screeches into a space. I check my rearview one more time, and the black Yukon is still behind me. Once I park, there's a still, pregnant moment where we all brace ourselves for the onslaught.

Then we unbuckle and step out of the car.

Layla heads directly for Roxanne, who seems to be giving her rapid instructions. The guys and I all gather at the side of the Yukon and wait.

First, a couple of guys from the football team I don't know very well climb out of the back seat, then reach in to move their seats aside. They have a small amount of blood on them, and their expressions are heavy with grief. Amber and Justin, Jeremy's twin, emerge slowly from the third row. They're covered in blood, some of it already dry and brown. Amber's face is tear stained, her eyes haunted, and she looks as if she's not really even there. Justin pulls her to the side and wraps his arms around her, his eyes red-rimmed.

The security officers roll a stainless steel gurney up to the car and climb in, carefully removing Jeremy's body, the knife still protruding from his back.

"Stop, please," Layla steps forward, her voice rough. She leans in and whispers to the officers, who nod. One of them removes the long silver knife with a gloved hand, then drops it in a clear plastic bag. Reddish-brown blood smears the inside, and he seals it up before handing it to her.

Now, of course, they're able to gently turn Jeremy on his back, and they cover him with a sheet.

Another officer has kept the Westley's on the other side of the vehicle, so they didn't witness the removal. Now they're able to come forward, and the wail Jeremy's mother releases upon seeing his body rivals the noise that Amber made when he died. I know without a doubt both sounds will haunt my dreams for a very long time.

Layla hands the bagged knife to Roxanne, then goes to speak to the Westleys. She gestures Amber and Justin over as well; her face heavy and lined with sadness, making her appear much older than eighteen.

"I can't express to you how sorry I am that this happened. I needed to leave pack lands on official pack business, and Justin and Jeremy volunteered to accompany me. I had no reason to believe it would be deadly, but I was hesitant to travel alone.

"Jeremy saved my life. He jumped in front of a knife meant for *me*. I'm unable to thank him, but please accept my gratitude, as your alpha, for his sacrifice. I am in your debt."

The twin's mom sobs heavily into Elliot Westley's shoulder, and he remains upright, eyes red but his face proud, as he nods his acknowledgement.

Layla steps forward and wraps her arms around both Amber and Justin, who peel apart just long enough to let her in. The security officers wheel the sheet-covered gurney past them, heading for the building.

Layla whispers something to Amber and Justin, who both nod, before she steps away. "We'll hold a ceremony for him at tomorrow night's run, and it would be my honor if you'd allow me to acknowledge his sacrifice at the homecoming festivities in front of the entire town."

Elliot Westley nods once more before his eyes stray to the gurney, disappearing into the building.

Eventually, people drift away, and Layla speaks to everyone personally before they depart. Finally, it's down to Roxanne, Derrek, Layla, and Milo, Jared, and me.

Roxanne still holds the knife in its plastic bag. The other guys and I are lounging against my car. When Layla shoots me a meaningful glance, I elbow the other two to get their attention and we go stand beside her.

Despite the exhaustion on her features, her expression is no longer sad. Right now, it's scary calm. The feeling that something is about to happen thickens in the air.

"Hey Derrek?" Layla calls out to him in a steady voice. He looks up from his phone. "Yeah Lex?"

"I just need to ask you a couple questions before we all go home, if that's okay."

"Sure." He tucks away the phone and flips his messy hair out of his eyes. "What's up?"

"This is the knife that we pulled out of Jeremy's back. You said it's spelled, correct?"

He nods. "That's right. It's imbued with magic that prevents normal healing. It'll require magic to heal wounds made with it."

"Is it dangerous for a non-witch to possess?" Layla keeps her voice gentle, clear, but non-judgemental.

"No, you're fine. Just don't nick your finger with it."

"And you know this because?"

He gulps, his smile dropping slightly. "It's mine. I mean, it used to be mine."

"Why would you own a knife like this?"

Now he looks distinctly uncomfortable. "Well, it was given to me. I didn't want it, so I gave it back."

"I see. So that's why Azalea said she wanted to give it back to *you*. Is she the person you got it from before you gave it back?"

"No. They must have given it to her."

"Why?"

Derrek shifts his weight from one foot to another. "I don't know. I wasn't there. It was after I was in LA."

"Okay. So what did Azalea mean by 'finish the job'?"

The older man goes completely still. "I'm sorry, what?"

"Azalea, before we left, said, *'if you decide to grow a pair and finish the job, the pack would welcome you back.'* What did she mean?"

I exchange a glance with Milo and Jared, and they both appear just as confused as I am.

Derrek is sweating bullets at this point, unable to keep still at all. He crosses his arms over his chest and shrugs, trying to laugh but coming up short. "I mean, I don't really know. She's always been a little nuts."

Layla's voice drops to a dangerous tone. "Don't lie to me, Derrek. Or should I say *Leaf*? Assume I already know the answer."

He holds her gaze for a long moment, then drops his head to his hands and sighs heavily. "Okay. The truth— the *whole* truth—is that Pack Montrose sent me to find and kill the Harridan heir."

"You piece of shit, I *knew* it!" Jared growls, already stepping forward with fists clenched.

"Jared, stop." Layla rolls smoothly into the alpha command like second nature. "No one touch him. I want to get the full story, because he's been telling me everything in bits and pieces and it hasn't made a bit of sense until now."

Jared backs up but continues to glare daggers at Derrek. I never particularly liked the guy, but I never hated him as much as Jared did. Now, however, white hot fury like I've never experienced boils in my veins. I'm able to move, but I know that if I move against him, the alpha command would restrain me. I focus on remaining still.

"The *whole* truth, Leaf." Layla's voice is flat, emotionless, as she prompts him to continue.

Derrek's eyes close as he pulls in a steadying breath before continuing. "Everything I told you about growing up was true, Lex. I didn't have much magic. My mom hid me from the pack. But they grew suspicious. They were asking for a demonstration of my powers. So my mom dug through Grannie's old spell books and found one filled with blood magic spells.

Essentially, the spell promised that if you vanquish your enemy, you could use their blood to enhance your powers. My mom told me it was my only way of coming into my powers. Otherwise, I'd be kicked out of the pack. So I accepted the knife, and I went to LA— that's where they said the runaway heir was hiding.

"I was looking for your *mom*, Lex, and I never found her. You've got to believe me. I didn't know anything until I saw a news piece about their car crash and their surviving daughter going into foster care. I recognized her face—how could I not? So now I had only one option: I had to pivot. It took some work, but I got a job with Child Protective Services and figured out where you were being fostered. And then I just had to wait for an opportunity."

"You sick piece of shit," Jared mutters under his breath.

Even Roxanne looks disgusted, the bloody knife clutched in her hand.

"So the night we met, you were going to attack me? Use my blood to get powers?"

"No! No, I swear. The more I watched you, the more I knew I could never do it. You were just a kid who knew nothing about this world. I felt a connection to you—we were both two people who didn't fit, who had no one. By the time you ran away, I'd already decided I couldn't go through with it. But I couldn't go home, and I couldn't leave you to get attacked, or worse, on the streets. You'd already gone through too much. So I intercepted you, got you to trust me, and mailed the knife back to my mom, telling her I was never coming back."

I don't know what to think. My heart is conflicted, with one part of me wanting to rip him to pieces for all the duplicity and deceit—exactly what we've always been told Pack Montrose was like.

The other part of me almost sympathizes with him. He can't help how he grew up, and when it came down to it, he made a different choice.

Layla stares at him, unmoving, for a long, painful moment. "So, how did this knife end up in my chest four years later?"

Derrek's pleading expression melts to absolute horror. "You can't think I had something to do with that? It was Azalea! She hunted us down. I did the best I could to shield us. My weak magic could barely help me manipulate people to provide us protection, or look the other way occasionally. I had no idea they'd send Azalea after you. When I left, she was supposed to be a dud."

"A dud?"

"A magical dead end. She displayed no powers. That's why the pack pinned their expectations on me. Typically, it's the first female child in the family, but between my mom and my aunt, they each only had one kid. Azalea presented with a complete lack of magic."

"So what changed? Because she clearly has magic now."

He sighs heavily. "If I had to guess... I would say she killed her mother. For the blood magic spell."

"I thought you said that was if you vanquished an *enemy*?"

"I believe Azalea considered her mother an enemy. With no magic to speak of, she was a complete disappointment to her mother. She treated her pretty terribly, growing up. I suspect my aunt was trying to punish her into manifesting, like some sort of gross tough love. In the end, I suppose she got what she wanted."

"So she's the one who attacked me in LA."

"Yes. I felt her magic. I guessed it was someone coming after you. I summoned enough power to force her off of you and keep her at bay until there were witnesses and she had no choice but to run. But I didn't get there in time to stop her, and I couldn't heal you." His voice crackles with emotion.

"And you're the one who told my uncle where I was."

"Yes. I told you, I knew that knife. You needed magic to heal, or you'd have died in that hospital. I had no other choice. I swear Lex, I would have kept you hidden, safe, forever, if I could." His voice hitches, then drops. "I'm sorry."

A heavy weight pressed on my chest, and I can't imagine how Layla feels. Her expression is frighteningly emotionless.

"I'm sorry too, Leaf. I really am. But it's time for you to go. Please leave Smoky Falls and don't come back."

Layla doesn't spare a backward glance, just turns and says, "let's go home," to me and the guys, then climbs into the passenger seat of my Grand Cherokee.

236

I raise my eyes to Roxanne, and she tips her chin toward Layla. "Go on, I'll finish up here and meet you guys at home."

We pile into the car, and no one says a word as we start up the long, winding path to Harridan House.

Chapter Twenty-Three

LAYLA

~

I know the guys sense my emotions—on some level, if not the same way I can sense their emotions—but there's no way I can convey the devastation I feel in the wake of today's fiasco. I take a shower and we have dinner, then watch a movie no one actually pays attention to.

And I know they're just trying to be here for me. If I told them exactly what I needed, they would do it, no questions asked.

The problem is, I don't know what I need.

I want them close at the same time I want my space. I enjoy their comfort while simultaneously feeling smothered. I can't make up my mind, and of course there's no way for me to really make them understand how I feel.

Because in order to do that, I'd have to confess that yesterday afternoon I was making out with a man who was sent to kill me.

And I just can't bear to see the betrayal in their eyes.

So when I feel like it's late enough, I ask them to go home.

Roxanne rustles me up a prescription to help me sleep, and I escape from reality for a few blissful hours.

When the morning comes I'm still not ready to face it, not ready to face them.

So I roll over in bed and text the guys, and Roxanne, that I don't feel well and I'm skipping class. Of course the guys offer to keep me company, and I turn them down, promising I'll see them tonight at the ceremony for Jeremy.

Roxanne planned it all out. Apparently they have a special honor for people who die protecting the alpha. We'll hold it at the run tonight, in front of the pack, in addition to the more public appreciation during the town festivities.

And I am really, truly grateful to Roxanne for handling all the arrangements. I can't process how Jeremy so willingly laid his life down to protect me. It was just a couple of weeks ago he was backing Amber's claim to challenge me as alpha. A month before that, he attacked me himself.

But I do have a better understanding of what it really means to be part of a pack. They needed me to

prove myself worthy, and once I did, the loyalty wa
unflinching.

Even in the face of a magic-imbued knife.

I can't say the same for Derrek.

As soon as the guys left last night, I lay in my bed
and cried. Heavy, painful sobs, and yes, some of them
were for Jeremy, but more of them were for me.

I only cried once after my parents died. I cried in
shock and anger, in fear and guilt. But when it came
time to grieve them, I couldn't bring myself to do it. My
eyes were dry at the funeral, and in the foster home, my
tears never escaped, no matter the humiliation or
shame. On the streets I was Lex, a tough street kid, and
I couldn't afford to be sad or emotional. You can't show
weakness in the wilds or you become the prey.

But here, in this place, all of my carefully built walls
have crumbled down, and I find myself overwhelmed
with grief.

So last night I cried for my parents. I cried for the
childhood they deprived me of, both as a beloved
member of this pack, and as a loved daughter with
adoring parents. I cried for the girl who got attacked by
a literal witch on an LA street, her arms cut to ribbons
and chest stabbed with a magical knife. The scars
itched when I thought about it, and I rubbed them
beneath the heavy fluff of my duvet as I cried some
more.

I cried for the guilt of having three fated mates but
still wanting another man, for the hurt I'm going to
cause them again and again. And I cried for the girl

whose hero was nothing but a villain who lied to her at every turn.

Because she loved him, and he broke her heart.

Derrek tried to text me last night, and I blocked his number. I shed some tears for that, too.

And so now, with bright midday sunlight streaming into my room, I've finally run out of tears. I understand the feeling of being all cried out; I couldn't shed another tear if I wanted to.

Of course, it could just be dehydration, but a part of me knows I've spent my grief, and it's time for me to stop wallowing and do something about it. My head and my heart are heavy, and I would like nothing more than to lie here for days, but the pack is depending on me to lead them. In order to do that, I have to get up.

And eat something, because I'm starving.

I shoot Roxanne a text, and within twenty minutes there's a knock at my door, Daphne rolling in a cart with silver-domed dishes.

She doesn't comment on the state of my pink and puffy eyes, or my absolutely insane bedhead. She just smiles at me brightly, producing a tray that she settles over my lap and starts loading with dishes. I almost manage to find another tear when I see what she's brought; it brings up a wave of nostalgia, memories of when I was sick as a child. Homemade chicken noodle soup with wide noodles and carrot slices, a bowl full of oyster crackers, and apple juice.

"Chef thought this would fix you right up." Daphne fluffs a pillow for my back with a smile. "But when you're finished, Susan sent this up as well." She sets a small plate of the special cookies and a mug with an ornate ceramic cover on the nightstand. "She reckons you could use a pick-me-up."

"Thank you, Daphne. Tell them all I really appreciate it."

"Of course, miss."

She bustles out, leaving the rolling cart out of the way, and I take a hesitant spoonful of soup.

It tastes exactly the same as what my mom made when I was little. I finish the entire bowl, splitting the individual oyster crackers open one at a time, just like I did as a kid.

And, sure enough, the special addition from Susan is her famous hot chocolate. The ceramic lid kept it hot, and a warm, glowy feeling fills my chest while I sip it.

Once again, I'm caught between my past and my new life. Soup from my childhood, cocoa and cookies from here.

And they're both equally comforting. They both bring warm memories of being with someone who just wanted to take care of me. And I realize that the soup I associate with my mom is probably a family recipe handed down to her, from my grandmother. Or at least from the family chef before William.

So perhaps I need to set aside the selfishness that fueled my tears last night. Maybe what Shuya said is the best advice she could have given me: Life isn't fair.

Being the alpha of Smoky Falls is a privilege, and it comes with a hell of a lot of responsibility. Despite the love and admiration of almost everyone in this town, I have been desperately searching for a way to get out of it.

And because of that, because of me and my need to be selfish, someone is dead.

I finish the cocoa and check the time on my phone; I still have several more hours before I need to get up and start preparing myself for the ceremony tonight. From now on, I have to be the alpha this town needs, the leader they deserve. I can't be an eighteen-year-old girl who only thinks of herself. The position comes with heavy responsibilities, but it also comes with support, in the form of my fated. They're meant to help me carry the load. But it's up to me to accept them. I have to stop thinking of myself as an island and start truly becoming part of the pack. I owe them the same respect and faithfulness they've shown me.

Derrek is gone, and the past is the past.

So I settle back into the warm bed and close my eyes, resolved to emerge from this cocoon of blankets like a butterfly.

Soon enough.

Chapter Twenty-Four

LAYLA

~

Nerves swim in my belly as I gaze out at thousands of solemn faces. My fated are on the stage with me, as is Roxanne, and Amber, Justin, his parents, and all the guys who were in the other car. I have their names on a piece of paper clutched in my hand—I still don't know half of them.

Last night's ceremony in the clearing had been different. We spoke Jeremy's name, thanked his spirit for his sacrifice, and honored him for protecting me. And when we ran as a pack, there was no playful yipping, no side races or weaving through the trees. We ran as one, a single unit. We returned to the clearing all together and howled a long, mournful cry until the hour was up and we had to shift back.

Tonight, the festive atmosphere is at odds with the somber truth. The entire town square is filled with people, adorable fall market booths lining the sidewalks in every direction. But I need to do this. I need to show the entire pack that I understand my duties to them as an alpha, as protector of this town.

The words want to stick in my throat, so I clear it and force myself to begin. "Hi," my voice is shaky and the microphone squeals. "For those of you who haven't yet met me, I'm Lilliana Harridan. My family has been a part of this community since the founding of Smoky Falls." I pull out the prepared speech and smooth the crumples I made in the paper before continuing. Roxanne stressed to me I needed to stick to the script, as there would be out-of-town visitors here for the festival.

But the pack could read between the lines.

"Even though my family has been here for generations, I'm relatively new to the area, and the dangers the wilderness presents. A couple of days ago, this group of my peers risked their lives to save mine. One paid the ultimate price.

"I know it's an odd choice of timing, but I just wanted to express, in front of the entire town, my gratitude to Jeremy Westley for saving my life. His sacrifice can never be repaid, and I am forever grateful." I pause as the crowd murmurs, the sounds of Jeremy's mom sniffling behind me. "I must also thank everyone involved…" I run down the list carefully, pronouncing each name correctly and not giving any more emphasis to my fated than I do to anyone else. "I couldn't ask for a more caring or generous community, and I hope to give back and honor you all for a very long time."

Applause builds like a wave from the sea of people below the stage, and I smile brightly, then pass along the line of people behind me, shaking all of their hands and accepting a few hugs, before I'm able to descend the stairs. My fated follow me down, and when we're finally out of view from the crowd, I accept their warm hugs of comfort.

"You did great, Layla." Jared grins. He's actually put on a button-down shirt for the occasion, although it's worn open under his jacket and over the ubiquitous t-shirt.

"Perfect," Landon agrees, his soulful eyes warm.

"I think we'll make a politician of you yet, Lex." Milo's signature half-smile curls his lips. "Do we need to find some babies for you to kiss?"

"Ha ha, you're hilarious," I roll my eyes. "Roxanne said after the announcement, I'm free to enjoy the festival. Where should we start?" I look around the group expectantly.

"Well, Landon and I have somewhere to be, so you two go on." Jared tips his chin at Milo before pulling me into another hug. "Just don't do anything we wouldn't do, gorgeous," he whispers, planting a soft kiss on my lips that sends a warm reverberation straight to my core.

"Okay," I reply, a little confused. I thought we were all spending the evening together.

Landon pulls me into a hug. "Bye, Layla," he

murmurs, cradling my face in his hands and kissing me in that sweet and sultry way that shoots electric tingles across my skin.

"Bye," I echo, flushed and breathless.

Both boys grin at me once more before sauntering off into the crowd.

My eyes cling to them until they disappear among the festival-goers. Then I turn to Milo.

"I thought we were all hanging out together?" I ask, lifting an eyebrow.

Milo, always the individual, wouldn't blend into the crowd if he tried. Instead of what appears to be a common local uniform of jeans and fleece jackets, Milo is wearing a long grey wool coat over black dress pants and shiny leather shoes. It sets off his black hair and enhances his bright blue eyes, and the guy looks like he just stepped off the pages of a magazine in New York.

"Well, we realized that it's hard for you to feel closer to us as individuals if we're always with you as the three musketeers. And since you've had some alone time with both of them in the last week, we agreed it was my turn." He presses closer, leaning in to say the last part in a low, sensual tone.

"Oh." My confusion turns to a flush of pleasure, remembering the one passionate moment I shared with Milo before the world blew up around me. "That sounds… perfect."

"This way, my lady." He offers me his arm, but I lace my fingers through his instead, and his casual smile widens, a hint of color reaching his cheeks.

We wander the festival for a while, pausing often to accept the greetings of pack members. Milo takes me to his favorite booths—naturally, we start with a drink from the Painted Moose—and we explore the best Smoky Falls offers.

I came prepared tonight, my purse stuffed with cash so I could patronize as many of the local businesses as possible. I let Milo buy my harvest spice latte, but after that I pay. He doesn't make a comment as I continue adding bags to the pile, just gently removes each one from my hands as soon as I've paid and loops it over his arm. Homemade fudge, fall crafts, honey from small family farms and blackberry jam, handmade soaps… I have no idea what I'll do with it all, but it feels good to share the wealth this town provides me with those who need it more.

The party is in full swing, a band playing bluegrass for the lively crowd, and I've barely visited a fraction of the booths when Milo clears his throat. "Lex, are you having a good time?"

Hearing that name squeezes my heart, but I smile up at him. "Of course, why?"

Color flushes his cheeks again. "Well, I don't want to drag you away if you're enjoying it, but I sort of planned something for us to do… alone, tonight."

My heart thumps in my chest, and my throat is suddenly dry. "Oh, yeah?"

"Yeah, I mean… just when you're ready to leave here, I don't want to go until you get your fill. I know it's your first time and there's a lot to see."

Tingles run up my spine, curiosity about what he could have planned filling me up and dampening the colors and sounds of the festival. Something tells me that if Milo planned it, it's special.

"I'm ready to go," I say, almost shyly. I keep remembering when he grabbed the back of my neck and kissed me, wondering if that's about to happen again, soon.

"Excellent. Right this way." He gestures with the hand laden with my purchases, and we veer away from the town square.

Away from the heat of so many bodies, not to mention fragrant steam from the food sellers, the fall breeze is a good deal sharper, biting at my cheeks. I'm grateful for the heavy cover of my hair now, keeping my neck and ears warm. Milo's collar is up, but the tips of his ears are red from the cold, and both of our breath appears like ghostly frost in the streetlights. Even my warm coat doesn't stop the cold from creeping in. I wonder how far we'll have to walk, even as I realize I don't know where we're going. It's still rather early. Perhaps he made reservations at a restaurant somewhere.

It's not until he reaches into his pocket and a nearby car beeps, lights flashing, that I know our destination. The trunk on a sleek, gunmetal grey car with blacked-out windows pops open, and Milo deposits my bags inside.

"Allow me," he passes to the passenger side, opening my door and making sure I'm settled before closing it gently. I sink into the leather seat, heat blasting, and buckle up while he walks around the back, closing the trunk before he climbs in the driver's seat.

"Milo, is this your car?" I ask, confused.

"Yeah," he replies. "It's a couple of years old," he adds, almost apologetically.

The interior is spotless, and the car smells like freshly treated leather. "It doesn't look very old. You take good care of it."

"Thank you." He grins, pulling a u-turn in the street and driving away from town center. "The truth is I don't drive it very often."

"Yeah, I guess that's why I assumed you didn't have a car. You're always riding with Jared or Landon."

He shrugs. "I don't really like to drive, and they do. I prefer to drink my coffee and relax. Plus, I try not to flex on my friends. The car is nice, and I like it, but it was a gift from my parents."

"What do you mean, you try not to flex on your friends?"

"It's... a very expensive car, Lex. A bit more spendy than a Chevy pickup, as nice as Jared's is."

I try to draw up the memory of the winged logo I saw on the hood, but I'm not familiar with it. "I'll take your word for it," I reply instead. "So, are you going to tell me the destination of our mystery date, or do I just have to wait until we arrive?"

He chuckles. "It's not a secret. We're going to my house."

"Oh, okay." A thrill runs through me at the idea. I haven't seen any of the guys' houses. I barely remember meeting their parents before my manifestation, but we didn't have drawn out conversations or anything. It was more like a swift meet-and-greet, and I was so nervous it's all a blur. "Are your parents home?"

"Nah, they're down at the festival like everyone else. We have the place to ourselves."

We continue to drive toward the outskirts of town, the smooth road curving upward into the hills. I watch the dark scenery ahead, broken only by the bright white headlights. It's mostly trees, with an occasional drive veering off to the side as we continue climbing.

Eventually, the road levels out and ends at the top of a hill. We follow a drive lined with modern streetlights overhead, leading to a wide circular driveway in front of a thoroughly modern house.

It's all steel and glass, wood accents keeping it from becoming too sterile. It's not nearly as large as Peter Jean-Yves house, but far more stately in its own way. I didn't realize until now how much of Milo's personal style is tied to his family and upbringing. With a jolt of sadness, I realize there's a lot I still don't know about him.

He hops out of the car and walks around to open my door as I resolve to take advantage of the gift he's offering me tonight.

Time for just the two of us.

Chapter Twenty-Five

MILO

My pulse races through my veins when I step around the Aston Martin and help Lex out of the car. I have carefully cultivated my entire life for keeping people out. I'm always the calm one. I never lose my temper or get overexcited, and I don't invite people in. Literally and figuratively.

This is an incredibly vulnerable moment for me, and adorably, Lex has no idea.

She angles toward the front door, but I tug on her hand. "Nope, this way." I gesture to the narrow walk that curves around, toward the back of the house. From here it looks like one very high story, but as we walk along the path and start descending the hill, she can see it's actually three, artfully hidden in the hillside. Lex walks quietly beside me, taking it all in while we follow the wide, well-lit flagstone steps.

My parents have always had money, just like Amber's. The difference is, they aren't interested in the sort of ostentatious displays the Jean-Yves' prefer. We don't have a sprawling manicured park of a property with a mansion full of expensive antiques.

Not to say that our house and furnishings aren't expensive; they are. My family just prefers subtlety. Our property covers a lot of land, but it's almost exclusively forest. Our house is rather spartan compared to my friends, and honestly, I prefer to hang at their places whenever possible. It's warmer, cozier. I can relax. Even though it's home, I spend the majority of the time I'm here in my room, because that's the only place I'm really comfortable.

Well, that, and the backyard.

I took care to make sure everything was perfect before I headed into town. I don't really want Lex in the house; not because I think she'll judge us or break something, but because I don't want her to get intimidated by the starkness like all of my friends did. I want her to be comfortable here with me, which is why the back is the perfect place to start.

We finally turn the corner, Lex's tiny fingers laced with mine, and I know when she sees it; her grasp tightens and her delicious lips pop open. "Milo," she breathes, her steps slowing. "This is incredible!"

I can't keep the pleased smile from spreading across my face—this is exactly the reaction I was hoping for, and my pulse quickens. I shrug noncommittally. "It's not that much. But I'm glad you like it."

Her wide eyes turn to claim mine, the bright emerald sparkling. *"Not that much?* Come on, now I *know* you're messing with me."

My smile widens. "Okay, fine. But I wanted our first proper date to be special."

"Oh, Milo," she sighs, eyes returning to the scene laid out below. "It is."

The back yard is my favorite place in the house for a variety of reasons. First, I love the view. Built into the side of the cliff, our house looks over the entire valley that houses Smoky Falls, but the best view is from outside, under the stars. I also love the pool and hot tub, and on the rare occasions I have friends over, we typically head straight back here to lounge.

Tonight I've had gauzy curtains draped around the pergola, along with extra string lights besides the Edison bulbs that typically line it. The household staff moved the patio furniture for me, filling the space with a fluffy nest of comforters and cushions. Two outdoor space heaters are set up and already glowing, keeping the area warm against the chilly night air, and further out on the lawn I've rigged a large projection screen.

I escort Lex to the cozy space under the pergola, and she kicks off her boots before climbing inside and tugging off her jacket.

"Be right back." I kiss her hand before releasing it with a grin, and head over to the outdoor kitchen. After grabbing the heavy picnic basket, I return and remove my own shoes and coat, then spread our refreshments out on the blankets.

Lex just watches me with an adoring smile that makes my heart flutter and my throat catch. "I uh… I hope you like charcuterie." I stumble over the words, then dart away to start the projector.

The opening scene queues up, and Lex looks at me in surprise. "The Breakfast Club?"

"Yeah, haven't you seen it? It's a classic." Nerves hum in my blood, but I suppress the anxious response. I hope she doesn't hate it, even as I smirk at her like I don't care what she thinks.

"I used to watch this with my mom when I was little," she answers, her voice dropping slightly. "I haven't seen it in a long time."

Shit. "You want to watch something else? The world is our oyster. Or at least, all of Netflix."

"No! Milo… this is perfect. I love it." She settles back into a pile of cushions and peers at the food between us, sniffing. "Ok, which of these cheeses is the stinky one? Because that one's got to go. It smells like dirty feet."

A surprised chuckle rips from my lips, my chest expanding as I relax. "Hey, Roquefort is a delicacy, I'll have you know."

"Maybe for rats." She grimaces. "Seriously, it's strong. Does it even taste good?"

"Well, you're not going to like it if you hate how it smells. You've already decided you don't like the scent, so I think the flavor is going to be a fail."

"Then… can we chuck it?" Her hopeful expression

is teasing, but of course I don't want her to have to smell it if she doesn't like it.

"Your wish is my command." I fish the plastic wrap from the basket and remove the offending cheese from the tray, wrapping it tightly and tucking it back into the basket. "Better?"

Lex draws in an exaggerated breath and sighs. "Yes, much better. No more feet. Thank you."

We dig into the snacks, and I explain and name some things she doesn't recognize. Once we're done eating, I move the food aside so we can scoot closer. The low pile of cushions creates a comfortable backrest, and Lex nestles into my shoulder with a contented smile.

Her cherry vanilla scent fills my nose, and the effect is confusing. She calms and simultaneously excites me, and I'm torn between tucking the covers up around her chin and tugging her face to mine.

"Milo?"

"Yeah?"

"What are you thinking about?"

My heart thumps. Sometimes she says stuff that almost makes me feel like she can read minds, before I remember that she likely was sensing my emotions.

Forcing myself to breathe deeply and calm my nerves, I reply in a smooth voice, "Not much. Just thinking that I enjoy being here with you."

She sits up, bracing her weight on her arm, and staring at me with one eyebrow raised.

Shit. "What?"

"Is that all you were thinking about?"

"Thats the gist of it, yeah." A sweat breaks out along the back of my neck. "Why?"

"Because your heart is pounding a mile a minute."

Oh.

I swallow my nerves with a difficult gulp. "Would it make me somewhat… less cool if I admit that I'm just the tiniest bit nervous?"

It was the right thing to say. She leans in closer.

"Why are you nervous, Milo?" Her voice is a sultry whisper.

My heart races even faster, and instead of giving her a typical 'nothing bothers me' answer, I decide to keep on my honest kick. My tone is softer when I say, "Because you're here with me, alone."

"Why does that make you nervous?" She leans in even closer, and her warm breath washes over my lips.

My voice drops to a near-whisper. "Because you drive me crazy, but I'm trying to behave myself."

And that was apparently the *exact* right thing to say. Lex leans forward and kisses me, a repeat of our first—and only, up to this point—kiss, except this time she's the one grabbing my neck, pulling me closer, claiming me.

In a swift move, she straddles my lap, bearing down on me with insistent kisses, her fingers trailing over my shoulders and back, her hips moving back and forth, rubbing against my swiftly growing erection.

My trembling hands trail down her sides, seeking contact with her skin under the hem of her cropped sweater. As soon as my fingertip strokes the silky flesh of her ribcage she moans, biting my lip and trailing kisses away from my mouth and along my jaw.

Taking this as encouragement, I slide both hands up her sides, running my thumbs along the curve of her breasts and over the hardening peaks of her nipples. Just the sheerest layer of lace separates me from grasping them.

Desire, hot and fierce, is ripping through me now. "*Lex*," I murmur into her billows of soft curly hair.

She goes completely still, her entire body clenching in an instant.

Cue panic.

"Lex, is everything okay?" I lower my hands from her breasts and try to pull back. I want to see her face, get a feel for what's going on in her head.

"Don't call me that," she whispers.

"I'm sorry?"

She sighs, then pulls away to meet my gaze with sad eyes. "That name. Just, please don't call me that anymore."

A hard lump drops in my stomach. *Of course.* Because Derrek called her Lex, and after everything, it just reminds her of him. Not what I want her thinking about when we're alone together.

"I understand." I reach up and cup her cheeks, pulling her sad face down to kiss her tenderly. "I won't use it anymore. You'll have to give me a pass if I slip up once or twice, though. It's pretty deeply ingrained in my head."

She nods with a tiny smile.

"So, what should I call you, then?"

Her eyes are still sad, and it's killing me. "I suppose you should call me Lilliana. That is my *true* name, after all."

I lift one brow and tilt my head slightly. "Are you sure that's what you want, Lilliana? It's kind of a mouthful, if I'm honest. Lil-ee-ahhhh-nah," I test it out, exaggerating each syllable.

That draws a giggle from her. "Well, maybe not all the time. But I've got to get used to using it as my name. She may have been odd, but Shuya seemed pretty insistent that I have to claim my 'true' name in order to have any power, and I keep wondering if that includes what she said about breaking the curse." Her gaze was drawn away, lost in thought for just a moment while she spoke, but now it falls into sadness as her eyes meet mine once more. "Ignore me. It probably doesn't matter. It turns out I'm a pretty terrible judge of character, so I probably shouldn't trust her any more than I trusted *him*."

She doesn't need to tell me who she means.

I was reclining on the cushions, but now I sit up completely, which unfortunately moves Lex to sit on my legs instead of the much more interesting spot she occupied before.

"Le-Lilliana, I feel like I need to tell you something."

She searches my eyes curiously. "Okay?"

"I know I didn't say much about Derrek—aside from coffee and fashion, I tend to keep my opinions to myself, and I never wanted you to feel like I was questioning you. But truthfully, it wasn't that I didn't trust Derrek... I was *jealous* of him. I suspect it's the same for all three of us. You and he had a connection that we had wished for our entire lives, and then you're finally here, and he showed up and it felt like part of you was being pulled away from us when we'd just gotten you.

"But that doesn't mean you were wrong to trust him. I don't think you could have chosen any better, given the circumstances. I think, in every possible way, you are, and will be, a great alpha."

Her eyes fill with tears, and I search for a way to lighten the suddenly heavy atmosphere quickly. Nothing like tears to kill a make-out session.

I tilt my head coyly. "Ooh, should I call you Alpha?"

She snorts, and I continue, drawing her closer to me.

"Alpha, how beautiful you are." I press a kiss to her collarbone. "Alpha, how lovely you smell." I trail kisses up her neck, and her breath hitches. "Alpha, I-"

"Okay stop," she breaks out in a fit of giggles. "I can't. You sound like the big bad wolf. 'Grandma, what big eyes you have! What big ears you have!'"

A chuckle bursts from my lips—she's not wrong. "Hey, to be fair, that was little red riding hood who said that. The wolf is the one with the ears."

"Still. We've got to be able to come up with something else."

A scandalous thought crosses my mind, and I trail my fingers up to her shoulders and around her back. I press more kisses to her jawline. "Hmm, what if I *am* the big bad wolf?"

With a snarl I scrape my teeth on her neck, then pull her to my chest and flip our bodies, landing her back on the ground and myself above her.

She laughs in surprise, and I grin down at her, delighting in the sound. "You really are beautiful, Lilliana," I murmur, and this time when I move in to kiss her, it's slow and tender. "Lily," I murmur against her lips. "I like Lily."

"I like it too," she replies, breathless. Her fingers tug at the buttons on my shirt as we kiss, exposing my body to the night air before her hot little hands scrape down the planes of my chest, nails tugging at the skin. It makes me gasp in surprise, the sensation zinging across my body and igniting a deeper burn in my gut.

I settle on one elbow while we kiss, and allow my free hand to trail back up under her sweater, brushing over the mound of her breast before palming the soft handful gently. Lily moans against my lips, her fingers trailing around my body and digging into my back.

A growl rises in my throat, and she claws me harder.

I break away from her mouth and stare down at her with a coy smile. "If I didn't know better, I'd think you *want* me to be the big bad wolf."

She pinches her swollen lower lip between her teeth and gazes up at me with liquid eyes. "Maybe."

My heart was already racing, but now it's practically double time. "Okay, in that case, I think we need to do this properly. What does little red riding hood say?"

She giggles, a hint of nerves in the sound. "What big eyes you have?"

I position myself on top, straddling her hips, and slowly run my hands up her ribs to the cropped sweater. Fortunately for me, it has buttons. I take my time, easing each tiny button from its hole until her sweater falls open, revealing the pink, lacy confection beneath. Lily's breath is coming in shallow pants now, her chest rising and falling rapidly. I trail my fingers slowly down along the straps, stroking delicately across her lace-covered nipples, then dipping my fingers beneath the fabric to rub them over her hardened flesh.

She bites her lip in response, stifling a moan, and I lean in close, pressing my lips to her ear. "The better to see you with, my darling."

Withdrawing my hands from her bra and sitting back, I trail my fingers down across her stomach. "What's the next part that riding hood says?" I tug on the waistband of her jeans, holding her emerald gaze while I slip open the button and slide down the zipper.

"Um…" her voice shudders as my hand grazes the flesh below her belly button. "What big ears you have?"

My grin widens, and I switch to kneeling between her legs. Watching her response carefully, I tug on the waistband of her jeans.

Lily doesn't say a word, just holds my gaze and lifts her hips so I can remove her pants in one tug.

I try not to completely lose my mind when I note that her little panties match the pink lacy bra.

Goddess help me.

Instead, I crawl up her body and rest myself beside her, allowing my free hand to trail languidly over her exposed skin. The heaters keep it warm enough, but goosebumps rise on her creamy flesh everywhere I touch, from tracing the mounds of her breasts, down across her stomach, over her thighs, and then, ever so lightly, along the delicate lace band of her panties.

I watch carefully, for any sign she's uncomfortable, before I allow my hand to trail gently across the mound between her legs. Wordlessly, she parts her thighs for me, and my fingers travel further. Heat rises off her flesh, the fabric soaked to the touch. I press ever so lightly and her eyes close, a moan escaping from her parted lips.

Leaning in, I whisper, "The better to hear you with, my darling." Sliding my hand back to the waistband of her panties once more, I pause. "Lily… if you want, we can stop right now. It's entirely up to what you're comfortable with."

She looks at me sharply. "Of course, I don't want you to stop. I've been waiting for this since the first time we kissed Milo. Jesus, I thought *you* were the smart one."

That brings a startled laugh to my lips, and she chuckles too.

But the laugh quickly changes to a gasp when I slip my fingers under the lace and stroke her.

Her panting breaths become heavier, light sounds of pleasure ripping from her throat with every exhale. I move my fingers faster; they're slippery with her desire for me, which admittedly turns me on even more.

As if I could get any more turned on.

My gorgeous, clever mate is reclined beside me, in the dreamy glow of the love nest I built for us. Everything about her is perfect, from her wild dark hair to her creamy skin. In this moment, I want nothing more than to see her back arch in pleasure from my touch, hear the sounds she makes in the crescendo, and know that it's all my doing.

She's enjoying it, but we're not quite there yet.

I lean in to kiss her, withdrawing my hand from between her thighs.

Lily makes a disappointed little noise, which confirms that my next plans will be well received.

Pulling myself away from her once more, I kneel between her legs and begin kissing my way down the inside of her thigh, caressing the soft flesh with my fingers. "What's the next the part?" I murmur between kisses.

"Um…" she's so caught in the moment, I think she's forgotten our little game.

"In the story, Lily. What is the next thing red riding hood says to the big… bad… wolf?" I draw out the question, nipping her tender flesh with delicate little bites.

"Oh!" She gasps. "What big teeth you have." Her reply is light, breathless.

I reach down and slide my fingers beneath the band of her panties, tugging them while she lifts her hips obligingly.

It takes seconds to get them completely off. My entire body is on fire with excitement, but I force myself to move slowly, kissing her knees before I part them, spreading her thighs, gently kissing one and stroking the other. Until finally I have her spread before me, gasping in anticipation of my next move.

My mouth waters at the sight of her, gorgeous and perfect and desperate for my touch.

I stroke two fingers delicately over her sensitive flesh, then bring them to my lips and suck the taste of her while she watches. My eyes close, a rumble in my chest betraying just how much I'm enjoying finally getting a taste of her sweetness.

Lily's body moves beneath the hand that still holds her thigh, writhing in need, in desire, for me.

I pull my fingers from my mouth and smile, keeping my gaze locked on her brilliant green eyes while I lower myself slowly into position. My arms reach out, curling around her thighs as I settle onto my elbows.

Finally, when I'm inches away from my goal, I blow a breath across her exposed flesh. She shudders.

"The better to eat you with, my darling."

And then I feast on her.

I have to admit I've done this a fair few times; I'd consider myself a connoisseur of how to pleasure a woman with my tongue, sometimes with my fingers as well. No one from my pack, obviously, but I figured it was prudent to learn how to provide for my mate when she arrived. Jared's sporting events, while not really my scene, were a welcome opportunity to meet girls.

But nothing compares to the way it feels to share it with my fated mate. Every stroke across her flesh sends tingles through my body, and the taste of her, the smell of her, fills my senses.

I'm a man drowning in the ocean, and I can't stop drinking.

So when her body clenches and shudders beneath me, I tighten my grip and attack her with more fervent strokes, willing her to reach the pinnacle and tumble over the other side with me at the helm.

As her moans grow louder, mine do as well, my lips humming against her sensitive flesh and increasing every ounce of sensation I can give her.

And when she finishes, the earth-shattering gasp and cry that is both pain and pleasure in one, a deep, glowing feeling of satisfaction builds in my chest.

My movements slow, and her body goes limp beneath me as I extricate myself gently, sliding up beside her and pulling her tightly to my body.

She sighs, snuggling in to my chest and nuzzling my neck, her leg wrapping lazily around my hips and pulling me closer. "Thank you, Milo. For tonight... for everything."

My heart jumps, emotion clenching in my throat. I press a kiss to the top of her head. "You're welcome, my darling. I love you, Lily Harridan."

"I love you too, my Milo," she murmurs against my chest.

I squeeze her even tighter, and when her breaths slowly even out, I drag the comforter over us and settle back to watch her sleep, safe and peaceful, in my arms.

Chapter Twenty-Six

LAYLA

~

I wake, rested and glowing with the memories of last night's intimate moments. After snoozing through most of the movie, Milo restarted it to the point we stopped paying attention, and we finished the entire thing before he brought me home.

He said he loves me.

The thought pops up in my head at random times throughout the day, making me grin furiously every time.

Not to mention sudden graphic flashes of what happened *before* he said that.

The other two guys greet me normally, despite the teasing about Milo's date idea—which I defend him vehemently for, it was really romantic—but even they can't miss that something happened, something impactful. I can't count how many times I catch Milo's eyes, only for him to bite his lip suggestively and make me blush. Sometimes I get one up on him, licking my lips and watching with delight as his ears turn red and he goes all fidgety, then tries to act normal.

And just as with Jared, in the wake of our intimacy, the real, *emotional* kind of intimacy, the feeling I have when touching Milo has changed to a deep reverberation instead of electric tingles. Funny enough, he seems to be in a different tune than Jared's, as if they were two distinct notes. I test it out, holding both of their hands, and I can feel the difference.

We finally finish classes for the day, and Jared has to run off to prepare for the homecoming game, so Landon is walking me to meet Maxwell.

"Layla?" Landon's voice is concerned.

I glance up in surprise to see the worry in his gaze. "Yeah?"

"You okay?"

"Yeah, I just… was thinking. Milo really surprised me last night, you know? Like, it's not that he's rich—clearly I don't care about that—it's that he tries so hard to hide it."

"Yeah, he's been that way ever since we were kids. Jared and I—we're definitely not poor by any means, but we're not quite as well off as Milo's family. And I think he's really sensitive to it because he doesn't want to be associated with negative opinions, the way some other families are." He doesn't have to tell me he means Amber.

"She can't help that her parents have money," I reply in a low voice.

"No, and how they behave is not her fault, either. But I think Milo knows that part of Amber's persona is built up around the expectation people have for her family. Now we know her better, but Milo has always kind of just wanted to fly under the radar. He'd prefer if no one knew who he was."

"Yeah, I can see that. It's funny, I thought of the three of you, he was the one who always spoke his mind. And I guess, to a degree, he does. But also not exactly. He just... he really surprised me, that's all," I finish lamely, flushing again. I realize gushing about Milo is probably not high on the list of things Landon wants to hear from me.

Landon just smiles. "I'm glad you got to see the real Milo, just like you got to see the real Jared. And you know my secret, too. So I guess we're all gelling pretty well."

I nod, but don't say the thought that's floating in my head: it's still not the same with Landon. I know his secret, but all I've gotten are some audio recordings of him singing. And they're great, and I love them... but I'm desperate to see him play in person. To really see him open himself up to me.

I know it's only a matter of time before our connection deepens, too. I imagine the next step is claiming them at my alpha ceremony in mere weeks from now, and then... well, I guess that's it. A throb of emotion hits me in the chest like a hammer—I don't want any of these guys to end up cursed like me. To only leave pack lands for a day at a time? It's no way to live.

Indignation rises in my chest once again. There has to be a way out of it. There *has* to be.

Milo said he loves me, and he believes in me. That their apprehension was more about their jealousy of Derrek than the three of them believing I was wrong. Maybe it's *not* crazy to think I could find an antidote to this curse—or whatever the right word is. A cure? A solution? An anti-hex?

I have no idea where Derrek went after he left our lands. I only know he's gone. But I mull over the possibility of unblocking him and asking him to to introduce me to someone at Pack Montrose. Maybe there's someone there who wants to end this feud as badly as I do. I can't believe they just keep hating our pack for generations for no real reason.

Of course, I think about how much my pack continues to nurse their own resentments, and realize it's entirely possible they hate us just as much as the people in Smoky Falls seem to think.

Besides, I can't handle contacting Derrek. Not yet. It's such a raw wound, and I just want to ignore it until it heals itself and fades to an ugly scar on my heart like so many others.

So no, I won't be reaching out to Derrek, which leaves me just one option.

Shuya invited me to come back. She even promised to make lemon bars.

I know it's a risk—it's possible Azalea's spell will notify her of my arrival and I'll have very little time to ask my questions before I have to leave. It's also possible she set that warning system specifically for Derrek and has disabled it now. Or Shuya could have made her cancel it, too.

But I know that this time, I'm going alone. There's no way I'll endanger anyone else. And I know when I'll go—Sunday, in the morning after homecoming. Everyone will take a slow, lazy morning, and with any luck I can go and come back before they even notice I'm gone.

Perhaps Azalea likes to sleep in on Sundays, too.

A girl can dream.

∽

Landon

∽

I see Layla off with Maxwell—she'll meet us at the field for the game later—and head over to the quad to meet Milo.

He's sprawled out in the grass with his sunglasses on, soaking up the unseasonable warmth like a lot of other students. It's probably the last warm, sunny day we'll have this year. The leaves are turning rapidly in town, and up at Harridan House they're already more on the ground than still on the trees.

I plop on the grass beside him, and he greets me without looking my way.

"Hey."

"Hey," I reply. "You made quite the impression on Layla last night. Well done."

His half-smirk appears, but he doesn't reply.

"So... you want to tell me what we needed to talk about?"

Sighing, he sits up and glances around, gauging the proximity of the other students. "It's Lily."

"Lily?" My brows furrow as I try to think of someone we know named Lily.

"Yeah, Layla. She asked me to stop calling her Lex, so it's Lily now."

My brows raise in surprise. "Really? Why?"

Milo dips his head and looks at me over his dark glasses. "Why do you think?"

It takes me a minute, but I catch up. "Oh, right."

"Yeah."

"So, what about her?"

"I know she's putting on a brave face, but I know the curse really bothers her. She feels guilty about inflicting it on us, and she hates the idea of being tied to this place for the rest of her life. She's trying but, she's not really happy."

"She told you all of this?"

"More or less. Last night, we kind of... tightened our bond, and I can feel more of what she's feeling. I'm making educated guesses about why she feels what she does."

"I see. So what do you propose we do about it?"

"Well, I think we should revisit what the old woman said, Shuya."

I snort. "She didn't say much."

"True, but what she did say was important. She said the cure for the curse was right under our noses, but we were too blind to see it. She said Lily had to accept her true name—that was also part of how we landed on Lily, short for Lilliana."

"Okay… so definitely not much."

"Right, but I think we need to really start trying to work it out. What could be the solution that we're too blind to see?"

"You realize that this is one of those impossible riddles, right? 'Tell me the one thing you *can't* see and I'll give you a million dollars.' There could be a million things we aren't seeing."

"Yes and no. I think we can narrow it down, if we try. Like, we know it's about the curse. We know the curse affects us and the entire pack, but most especially, it affects Lily."

I gaze down at the grass between my knees, letting my vision glaze over while my brain works. "We should assume it's not something we *literally* can't see, but figuratively."

"Yes, exactly!" Milo taps my shoulder. "It's something we're unable to comprehend or think of because of our particular biases or perspective."

"Biases could be something," I admit. "When it comes to Pack Montrose we have pretty strong biases."

"True. But Le-, I mean, *Lily* doesn't. She's called us out on that more times than I care to admit."

"Also true. But everything she knows about Smoky Falls and Pack Montrose has been told to her *by* us, by people here. So you don't think that comes with an inherent bias?"

"Fair," Milo agrees. "So the likely solution has something to do with Pack Montrose, that our bias, being from Smoky Falls, is affecting."

"Seems most logical."

"So, what are our biases about Pack Montrose?"

I snort. "You mean, aside from the fact that they're selfish traitors who betrayed their own families because they wanted more than their share and heartlessly cursed our entire pack to get their way? Or that they killed our alpha out of cruelty and malice and even sent assassins to kill subsequent Smoky Falls alphas?"

"Yeah, there's a lot to unpack there."

"Tell me about it."

We both sit and consider in silence. The sun is hot on my shoulders, and I pull my sweater off to use as a pillow, sprawling out in my t-shirt on the grass. Milo remains sitting up, thinking. I can't imagine how hot the sun feels on his black shirt, but he doesn't seem to mind.

"What if we try to pick apart our narrative of what happened with the curse?"

Milo's voice is slow, thoughtful.

"Okay," I reply evenly. "Like how?"

"Well, say we choose just one supposed fact and assume it's wrong. That would mean we'd have to adjust the rest of our assumptions accordingly, right?"

"Okay… give me an example."

"Sure. What if… Pack Montrose didn't split from us because they were selfish or traitors. What if they split from us for a different reason, one that is less evil-sounding than that?"

I mull it over for a minute. "So if that were the case… you could make an argument that the curse was an unintended consequence of their attempt to free themselves from our pack… for whatever reason."

"Right, exactly! So if the curse wasn't intentional, then perhaps the death of Lily's great aunt wasn't intentional, either."

"That's a possibility. But the problem remains: we know they sent first Derrek, then Azalea, to kill Lily. So even if they didn't mean to kill Lilliana three generations back, them trying to kill Lily and her mom is still a constant. That doesn't change."

"Well, what if we assume it isn't Pack Montrose who sent them? What if the witches went rogue, or maybe someone in the pack sent them, but not everyone in the pack feels the same way or knows about it?"

I sit up abruptly. "This feels like it could go on forever. We can make up imaginary scenarios all we want, but it's just too much speculation and not enough fact."

"I know," Milo agrees, pulling off his glasses and

rubbing his face. "But there's something here, something that doesn't quite add up. I can feel it, teasing the back of my mind, daring me to sort it out. And for Lily's sake, I really want to." He looks up and holds my gaze. "I... I love her, you know? I want her to be happy here, with us. Whatever it takes."

My throat is thick; it's hard to swallow. I don't think I've ever heard Milo use the L-word. Not even about his own parents. Not even when we were kids, and we 'loved' random shit like BMX bikes and anime.

"I know what you mean." My voice is hoarse when I finally force the words out. "I'll think about it some more, but I'm getting nothing right now. Let's go get something to eat. We need brain food. Do you need to change before the game?" I side-eye his khakis and loafers. "The temperature is going to drop tonight."

"Nah, I'm fine." He stands, brushing off his pants. "I have some stuff in the back of Jared's truck for tonight. You want Badger's?"

Chapter Twenty-Seven

LAYLA

~

And just like a 90s teen movie, the day of the big dance has arrived.

The football game last night wasn't that much more crowded than normal—I think the town pretty much turns out for all the games regardless—but there was definitely more excitement in the air, higher stakes on winning. Naturally, our star player—my mate—led us to victory, and it was a night of triumph and celebration.

I suppose in some way, the entire household at Harridan House has adopted me as their daughter/sister/granddaughter, besides just being their alpha. I've seen makeover montages in movies before, but I've never seen so many people excited for me to experience something so outwardly benign. Mrs. Dowling has the maids hustling into my room when the sun is barely up, and after a quick breakfast I'm treated to an epic makeover.

Apparently Daphne's cousin owns the nail salon in town, so Cheri comes up to provide nail services in my suite before she opens up her shop. Not having ever experienced a manicure or pedicure, I'm left feeling both raw and picked at, and yet strangely pampered. I try to pay her but she won't hear of accepting money, so I resolve to patronize her in the future. I send Roxanne a text and she promises to put it on my calendar.

After my nails are polished and sparkling, Roxanne lines a pile of new skin products up on my counter and explains the order in which we're going to treat my skin. I'm really not feeling the need for it, so she threatens to haul me into town for a full spa facial, and we settle on doing it together in my bathroom instead.

At some point, after the hurt from her deceit faded, our relationship warmed again. It's still not exactly maternal, although Roxanne is twice my age. But she definitely feels like an attentive older sister, or an adoring aunt.

And I hate to admit, but we have fun painting the clay masks on each other with tiny fan brushes, trying to follow the fifteen gazillion steps this at home facial kit she bought requires. I knew Roxanne loved to shop, but I didn't know she was obsessed with Korean beauty products. She promises to show me her stockpile at another time, and when I ask what the weirdest thing she's bought is, she admits to owning a 24 karat gold Hello Kitty moisturizing mask.

It's amazing how people can continue to surprise you. I always assumed she loaded me up with those products because she thought I wanted them. I had no idea that behind the very practical facade, Roxanne is secretly a hoarder of kitschy Korean pop beauty.

We break for lunch, and then things get serious. I haven't given a thought to how I'd do my hair, but Roxanne already has a plan. I take a shower and leave my dripping mane in her hands, trying to relax instead of focusing on the nerves zinging through my body. Roxanne's hands are gentle, and she combs products through my hair, then gently dries it a chunk at a time on a low setting with a lot of scrunching, and finally she begins pulling sections up and pinning them.

Naturally, she's got me in the suite, so I can't see what's going on until it's finished. Her eyes glow with anticipation as she steers me to the bathroom, and I finally get to see the artful updo she's created, complete with a tiara that shines like diamonds in my dark hair. Instead of a frizzy, wild mane, she's worked my hair into large, loopy curls that shine.

"Wow, Roxanne, it's fantastic!" I turn my head in different directions, admiring her work before I catch her face in the mirror. She's gazing at me fondly, her eyes half-filled with tears, and my heart lurches. I turn and pull her into a hug. "Thank you for everything," I murmur. I can't bring myself to say more. Emotion is clogging up my throat.

She squeezes me back and half-sobs, half-laughs. "Okay, stop, no crying! It'll make your face puffy and undo all the work we just did on your skin, girl. We don't have time for that. The boys will be here soon."

We get settled in to the bathroom so Roxanne can do my makeup—she insists I'm not getting away with half-assing it tonight, so I just let her go to town, and finally she helps me into the gown she picked out.

It's not a full, huge princess gown, but it definitely has an elegant corset-style top and a fuller skirt that flares out from the smallest point of my waist. The entire thing is a silvery-purple confection, and even I can admit it's stunning. Roxanne helps me slip on a pair of low, sparkling heels that are insanely comfortable, and then she finally spins me toward the full-length mirror so I can see the ultimate result.

And I fully, honestly, don't recognize myself for a solid ten seconds. The girl in the mirror has dark hair like me, but it's a pile of silky midnight ribbons. Her pale skin is practically glowing, and her bright green eyes sparkle like glimmering emeralds compared to the dark wash on her lids. She's not a skinny girl with bony shoulders; her feminine body fills out the elegant dress and emphasizes her womanly shape.

"I look like a princess," I breathe. "I... I don't know what to say," I admit, still searching the mirror for signs that this is actually me.

Roxanne steps up behind me, resting her dark chin on my shoulder. "I'm glad you can finally see it, Layla. We've all known for quite some time." She grasps my shoulders gently to turn me so she can hold my gaze, and adds, "But not a princess; a queen."

I reach out and wrap my arms around her, hugging her tightly. "Thank you," I whisper again.

"It's my pleasure, Layla." She beams as she steps back.

"Lilliana, please. Or Lily," I stammer. "I've been told I need to accept my true name, so I might as well start now."

Understanding flashes in Roxanne's dark eyes. "Lilliana, then. I'll let the staff know. Are you ready?" She checks her phone. "I believe all the guests have arrived."

"Sure," I say, then glance around. "Does this thing come with a purse? I need somewhere to put my stuff."

"Even better," Roxann grins, "It has pockets." She parts the fabric at the sides and helps me load the necessities into the deep hidden pockets, then walks with me down the long hall. I can hear low music and the rumbling of lots of voices echoing up from the ground floor already, and my stomach twists with nerves. I head toward the elevator, but Roxanne gently steers me toward the stairs.

I glance at her in panic. "Do you want me to trip?"

"No, I want you to have the opportunity to make a grand entrance. Even if you never do it again, a girl should have one 'gliding down the stairs to the admiring crowd' moment in her life. This is your moment, girl."

"More like falling down the stairs," I mutter, and the

panic rises in my throat. But some part of me is excited —it's literally a fairy tale come to life, and Roxanne has orchestrated the entire thing for me to experience it. So by god, I'm going to do it.

I hitch up a handful of satiny fabric to clear my feet and grasp the banister with a sweaty palm. Shooting one more panicked glance at Roxanne, I catch her 'thumbs up' gesture before she darts toward the elevator. Knowing she and my mates, not to mention a good portion of Smoky Falls, will be waiting downstairs for me, I suck in a deep breath and start my descent on the curving staircase.

My heart pounds against my ribs, each beat feeling like it's attempting to actually break free. My hand leaves a sweaty trail on the banister, and I spare a guilty pang knowing that Daphne or Mary will have to clean it. But I focus all my energy on not tripping as I follow the curve into view of the crowd below.

There's so many people, and as one, they fall silent when I appear. A sea of faces stares up at me, and my throat clenches, panic rising and cutting off my air supply. Somehow, this feels far more vulnerable than standing on the stage last night.

I try to smile confidently, and as my eyes wash over the crowd, I realize they are all beaming back at me. Happy, proud, admiring—I open my alpha sense and finally see I'm surrounded by a wave of love and support—it eases my tension and I draw in a deep breath, continuing carefully down the stairs.

Light flashes in my vision, but I ignore it—my gaze

has finally landed on the three men waiting for me at the foot of the stairs, and now I can't look away.

Landon wears a basic black suit that hugs his tall frame, but the skinny tie and fitted pants emphasize the rockstar look. I'm starting to think Milo does it intentionally. Milo, of course, wears a black shirt under his gunmetal grey suit, and Jared—for whatever reason—went with an all-white tuxedo. It would almost be funny if it didn't look so sharp against his dark skin.

I'm just pleased he's not wearing a ball cap.

All three gaze up at me with the most adoring expressions, and I adore them right back. A phantom pang squeezes my heart, but I quickly shove it down and bury it deep.

Content now, excited to see them, I practically float down the rest of the stairs and greet them each with a hug and a kiss.

And now that I've made my grand entrance, the party picks back up in full swing.

It's hard to believe this isn't even the actual dance—this is just the pre-party for the pack members past their college homecoming years.

After my all-day makeover, I'm starving, so the guys and I head into the formal dining room immediately to eat.

The giant table is gone, replaced by a dozen smaller standing tables with a long buffet spread out along the wall. We fill plates, then select a spot to eat, and I take the utmost care not to spill on my dress.

"So, how long does this go?" I ask between mouth-fuls. "Like, when do we head into town for the dance?"

Milo shrugs. "Whenever we want, really. Techni-cally, the dance starts in half an hour, but people just show up whenever. There's no rush. The party goes all night."

A brief pang of guilt squeezes my heart; I don't want to be out too late, since I'm planning to sneak out early tomorrow to visit Shuya. Even though my plan is to feign exhaustion and leave early, I still want to enjoy the dance first.

But they don't need to know that.

Instead, I say, "Since it's my first proper dance, I'm kind of excited to get down there and check it out. Do you guys mind heading out after we eat? I don't care if we're unfashionably early."

Milo smirks. "Lily, you're the alpha. Whatever you do is never unfashionable. As soon as people know you're leaving, they will rush to follow you."

"Okay, good. But let's get another plate," I grin, polishing off my last canapé.

I was expecting to have to stop and talk to people constantly until we make our escape, but it seems as if the pack is content to allow me space for one night. Aside from proud or indulgent smiles as we pass, people leave us alone.

When I catch Roxanne's eye and let her know we're ready to leave, she produces a dark plum velvet cape to wear over my dress. The crowd surges gently around us, walking with us to the door to see us off, and I note several other young couples gathering their things in preparation to leave.

It appears Milo was right yet again.

We exit through the front doors, where Maxwell waits with a stretch limo that can accommodate far more than the four of us, and excitement flutters in my chest as we drive toward town.

This must be how Cinderella felt, finally in the pumpkin carriage, on her way to the ball.

I wish I could say that I'm cool, calm, and collected, but the truth is, the little girl inside of me is thrilled to be going to a dance in a fancy dress, just like a princess. All I want is to dance with my fated, surrounded by other members of my pack, and enjoy a night of carefree fun before it's back to reality early the next morning. I imagine us sweeping around a crowded ballroom; the guys taking turns spinning me expertly while my skirt flares out and the crowd watches with admiration.

I know the reality is there will probably be a DJ playing top 40 dance hits and it'll be a far less romantic and dignified style of dancing, but I'm happy to indulge the dream for a few moments longer.

Finally, we pull into the parking lot of the community center. It's not a squat, dingy building like the ones I knew in LA. This building is tall and elegant and looks more like a fancy hotel. It's backed by lush landscaping, and warm light emits from the glass doors.

The guys and I climb out of the limo, Jared providing a hand so I don't stumble, and we thank Maxwell before he drives off.

I stare up at the elegant sign welcoming us to the Smoky Falls Homecoming Ball, my heart fluttering like a hummingbird in my chest. The promise, the anticipation of this moment, is rich and glittering and I just want to breathe it in for a moment longer. Everything today has been perfect, and I can't wait to have yet another new experience with my fated.

We stand in a row, all facing the building, and I glance along the line to each of my fated, holding their gazes and soaking in the adoring smiles they wear just for me. "Are you guys ready?'

A horrifyingly familiar snide voice calls out from the trees, and my blood instantly runs cold. "Sorry, princess, but I don't think you'll be attending the ball this evening."

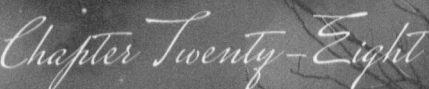

Chapter Twenty-Eight

LAYLA

Peter Jean-Yves steps out of the shadows, along with nearly a dozen other adults from my pack that I don't know personally.

I'm not sure what exactly he thinks he's up to—his aim is to stop me from attending the homecoming dance? It seems very cartoon villain to me.

"Peter, so nice to see you," I reply smoothly. "Did you take care of that little problem with your neighbors?"

He barks a harsh laugh, then affects an exaggerated bow. "As you commanded, oh high alpha." The others chortle, and my mates shift uncomfortably around me.

I keep my chin high and focus on making sure my

voice remains steady. "I'm glad to hear it. So if you'll excuse me, I have somewhere to be."

"Oh, I think you didn't hear me before. You won't be attending tonight."

A snort pushes from my nose. "And you think you're going to stop me? I thought you were smarter than that, Peter. What do you have against dances?"

His face contorts into a snarl. "I'm smarter than you realize, girl, but it's far too late. I have nothing against dances, just against spoiled, selfish Harridans that care nothing for the lives they ruin." The group of his supporters mutter their agreement.

My heart squeezes, and I try again in a gentler tone. "Peter, I'm sorry my mother rejected you. I wish I could change it. I know it was a cruel thing to do, and that she hurt you. But I can't take responsibility for her actions— I can only try to do better with the opportunity I have to lead the pack."

To my surprise, he bursts into a fit of laughter, and after a few seconds, the rest of his group does as well. "That's what you think this is about?" He sputters. "Your stupid whore of a mom? I thought *you* were smarter than that."

I bristle, and a low growl rumbles in the chests of my fated. They close ranks around me, all of them close enough I can feel their body heat. "You're a bitter man, and I'm sorry I can't help you. Why don't you go home and find something better to do with your time than harassing teenagers going to a dance?"

With my nose in the air, I turn, preparing to ignore any additional insults, and head into the building.

However, a crackle of power in the air is my only warning before something solid and invisible stops me in my tracks.

My lungs refuse to draw in air as if they've been stunned. There's nothing between me and the stairs that I can see, but I can't move forward. Every hair on my arms stands at attention, and I know the prickling sensation on my skin.

Turning slowly, I spot Azalea slinking out of the shadows behind the group of older men. She's in the same all-black getup she wore the last time we saw her.

"Witch," I spit. "You are not welcome here. Leave, now." My voice instinctively takes on the alpha double timbre, and she laughs with delight.

"Oh, little Harridan, you have no power over me, have you forgotten?"

Fury shoots through my veins like lightning, my wolf clawing to come out and attack her. "You may be right, but you're the only one. Take this-"

I begin to address all the pack members around me, both my fated and the other men, but my air is abruptly cut off as if an invisible hand is squeezing my wind-pipe. I claw at my throat, but there's nothing to grab.

Azalea makes a lazy hand gesture with a wicked grin on her blood-red lips, and the pressure on my throat tightens.

Peter and his cronies laugh with evil delight, and

after realizing there's nothing they can do to help me, my fated turn as one toward Azalea.

"Now, now boys, play nice," she taunts them, and the older men step between my fated and the witch. There's three times as many of the bad guys as my mates. They don't really stand a chance. The boys try to fight their way through and they land a few good punches, but in a matter of seconds, the larger group has them restrained.

At this point, the need for air is becoming painful. If I'm very still, I can draw in a tiny amount, just enough to keep me from suffocating. But it's like dying of thirst and receiving only one drop of water at a time—not nearly enough.

"What is wrong with you?" Jared shouts at the older men. "This is your alpha! Your duty is to protect her. How could you invite this witch into our territory?"

Four of the older men are keeping him at bay, pinning his arms behind him and forcing him to kneel in the filthy parking lot. I spare a thought for his white tux that is certainly ruined now.

"She's no alpha to me," Peter snarls. "She's born of a line that abandoned the pack—I don't care what you believe about the blood magic, there are ways to get around any spell. And we just happen to have one," he hitches a thumb at Azalea.

"Dad?" Amber's frightened voice calls out from behind me.

Unbeknownst to me, other people have arrived to attend the ball and discovered this bizarre scene. Me, bent backward awkwardly on my toes, barely able to breathe. The Montrose Pack Witch magically suffocating me, and my fated bloodied and forced to kneel at the feet of these traitors.

"It's time, Princess!" Peter calls to her delightedly. "Once Azalea here uses the Harridan girl's blood to break the curse, you'll finally be able to claim your place as alpha. I promised you'd have it."

Azalea's eyes dart nervously behind me. "Perhaps we ought to get this show on the road. There's more of them coming."

I reach out with my alpha senses, trying to gauge how many people have arrived and how they feel. If we have enough people who are loyal, we can overwhelm Peter's little gang.

And while it's not many yet, all of them are furious.

"No, Dad, I told you I don't want this! Layla is the alpha. Let her go!" Amber steps up behind me, and I feel her small hands touch my shoulder as if searching for some way to help me.

"Uh-uh, back away from her or I'll crush her throat completely. Right now she can breathe, if just barely." Azalea's warning is clear and threatening, and Amber takes her seriously, stepping away.

"Smart girl. Now, come along, Harridan, we have somewhere to be." The pressure on my throat eases just slightly, and a second force pushes me forward as Azalea turns to walk back into the trees.. My fated mates thrash against the men holding them, but can't break free. Every moment more members of my pack join the crowd behind me, and soon I know we'll have enough to overwhelm the group of troublemakers. It doesn't solve for the witch, but it's a start...

"That's far enough, Azalea." A male voice rings out from behind me, and the sound of it sets my pulse racing even faster.

Azalea turns to look at the new arrival, and her darkly delighted grin returns. "Cousin! I wasn't expecting to see you here."

My fated stare with wide eyes and slack jaws, but I can't turn to look. However, knowing that Derrek is here, that he's come back to help, gives me heart. I know he doesn't have much magic, but if he can help me just enough that I can issue an alpha command...

"Clearly," Derrek answers in a sarcastically flat voice. "Although I suppose Lex might say the same. What are you doing here, Azalea?"

"I'm just here to finish what our grandmother started," she answers in a baby voice. "The complete eradication of the Harridan line, the freedom from oppression for all these wolves. I was invited." Her tone changes to a snarl at the last word. "Somehow, I doubt you can say the same."

"Actually, he can." A deep voice I haven't heard in nearly two months reaches my ears. "As a member of the Harridan line, I'd say I'm uniquely placed to invite whomever I choose into our pack territory."

A gasp goes up among the crowd as they realize my uncle Dom has just appeared among us, after disappearing the night I manifested.

Azalea snorts. "Harridan or not, you're not the alpha, so you hold no power. I only need the girl."

"Well, I'm afraid you can't take her," Dom replies forcefully.

"Watch me," the witch snarls. With a flick of her hand, the pressure resumes on my back, forcing me forward. I stumble, trying to remain on my feet for fear of what would happen if I fell.

Suddenly, a swell of wind erupts around me, creating a cyclone that stings my eyes and forces them closed. I feel pushed and buffeted inside a narrow column that I can't escape, and the pressure on my throat increases, cutting my air supply off completely. I flail around helplessly, trying to escape a jail that's nothing but air as the darkness closes in around the edge of my vision.

Tears leak from my eyes, drying immediately in the gale force winds that bind me. As it typically is, the whole day was too good to be true. Cinderella's ball ended at midnight, and it looks like mine is over before it even begins.

Chapter Twenty-Nine

LAYLA

~

Just as I give up on ever drawing another breath, the pressure on my throat stops immediately, and my own personal hurricane disappears, leaving me struggling on my knees. I try and fail multiple times to draw in a full breath, achieving only thin, painful pulls of air accompanied by a horrifying croak emitting from my throat.

Many warm hands stroke my arms, my back; patting, rubbing circles.

"Come on, Lily, breathe!" Milo's voice is desperate.

My lungs feel like deflated balloons I don't have the power to fill.

"Gorgeous, you can do this!" Jared encourages, at the same time that Landon pleads, "Please, Layla!"

Instead of trying to fill my lungs, I settle for pulling in small sips of air, gradually drawing larger breaths as my fated huddle around, encouraging me. I'm desperate to know what's going on with Derrek and Azalea, my uncle, and Peter's rogue faction, but I need to get oxygen to my brain before I can process anything.

I don't know how long it takes; I know my fated are here, encouraging and protecting me, as I slowly draw in more and more air, and my heart gradually slows when I'm finally, painfully, able to pull in a full breath. My lungs seem better, but my throat still feels like a crumpled paper cup. My eyes open, and I stare at the ground, afraid to move my neck.

I try to speak but only manage to make a sound like a creaky door. Wincing, I try again, and force out the words, "Help... up... water," in a whispery approximation of my voice.

I hear a set of feet take off in the building's direction, and warm hands grasp my arms and lace between my fingers on each hand. The deep, comforting reverberations of Jared and Milo run through my body, one on each side. They lift me gently until I'm on my feet, and I turn my head carefully, testing for injury. Attempting to swallow, I realize there's what feels like a lump the size of a baseball preventing it. I reach a hand up to touch it, and feel nothing abnormal besides extremely hot skin.

"It'll heal, gorgeous, and quickly. You just need to give it some time. Landon went to get you some water. Are you okay otherwise?" Jared's dark eyes are filled with concern, his thick fingers gripping my hand tightly.

I nod carefully, then look around, shocked to discover we're alone. Tipping my head to the empty lot, I croak out, "where…?"

"Where is everyone?" Milo surmises. I nod again. "Derrek whipped up that tornado that cut off Azalea's hold on your throat. The second she realized she wasn't the only witch on the block, she took off running into the trees, and Derrek chased her. The rest of the pack surged on Jean-Yves and his cronies, and they ran off down the street. They all followed them… I'm guessing they won't get far."

A door opens and rapid footsteps approach. "Here," Landon is panting slightly, his voice breathy. He appears in my field of vision with a frosty water bottle, cracking the top and holding it out for me to drink.

"Take it easy, gorgeous," Jared cautions. "Just a little sip to make sure you don't choke. We don't know what damage she did to you."

The water is soothing on my tongue, and despite my desperate desire to chug it I follow Jared's advice, taking only a tiny sip before attempting to swallow.

I sputter, coughing, but a small trickle makes it past the lump. Jared pats me on the back and I gesture for more, which Landon obligingly holds up.

It takes a few more minutes, but I'm finally able to swallow down a few mouthfuls of water, and while painful, my throat feels as though it's functioning normally.

"Derrek?" my voice is a stronger croak now, more like a bullfrog than a squeaky door.

The guys exchange a glance. Milo begins, "Derrek…"

"Is right here, Lex." The man himself steps out of the shady clump of trees. "I'm sorry. I chased her as long as I could, but I didn't catch her. She had a car waiting at the edge of your pack territory."

I close my eyes and nod, swallowing painfully.

"Here, let me," he reaches toward my neck, and the guys step between us.

"Not on your life," Jared snorts.

"Guys," I croak, pushing at their shoulders. "Magic… help."

Derrek holds up his hands. "She's right. I just want to help heal her throat. I can speed up the process."

Slowly my fated step aside, and Derrek moves in closer. He's disheveled, rough looking, with several days of stubble and obvious signs of running through the forest like leaves in his wild curls. His eyes are bright, almost glowing green.

He lays both hands on my neck, one on either side, and studies my face seriously for a moment, then closes his eyes.

A warm tingle starts under his fingertips, spreading through my neck and deep into my throat, making me want to cough. I try to hold it in and allow him to work, and after a moment, he steps back. "There, that should be better. All I can do is speed up your natural healing a bit, but I was able to bring down some of the swelling."

I swallow again, and find it's much less painful than before.

"Thank you." My voice has become a papery whisper, but that's definitely an improvement. "How did you get... your magic?" I have to break up the question into two phrases as I draw a breath. That part is still hard.

Derrek sighs and runs a hand through his hair. "It's sort of a long story, Lex. But to really make a long story short, my powers were always here—my mom bound me when I was a child. I guess she was trying to protect me, keep me from ending up at the beck and call of the pack. When I turned up asking for help, she admitted it to me and unbound me. I've spent the last couple of days in what you might consider warlock bootcamp."

"Help for what?" I ask curiously, my breathy voice improving by the minute.

"Protecting you, of course. I knew Azalea would come after you. It was only a matter of time. And I didn't have the powers to protect you."

Something warm and glowing radiates in my chest. "Thank you," I whisper.

"You don't owe me thanks, Lex. And I don't expect your forgiveness. I know I have a lot to make up for. But I'm hoping you might find it in your heart to let me stay and give me my job back? I really miss the lectures."

A laugh pushes up from my chest, immediately making me cough as my lungs constrict. Milo rubs circles on my back until I can breathe normally. "I think that could be arranged," I whisper.

"Thanks, Lex."

"No prob, Leaf."

He groans. "I am never forgiving Grannie for telling you that name."

I resist the urge to laugh again—it was too painful.

A murmur of voices and footsteps on the pavement reaches me. I turn and see a crowd walking our way.

It's a strange sight; girls in fluffy dresses with fabulous makeup and carefully styled hair; guys with tuxedoes or three-piece suits, complete with high-polished shoes.

And all of them appearing as if they just rolled down a forested mountainside.

Upon catching sight of us watching them, a girl at the front lifts her poofy pink dress and starts running, her filthy, bedraggled blonde hair streaming out behind her. "Layla!"

Amber doesn't stop running until she throws herself into my arms, and I wince at the impact but wrap her tightly, anyway. "I'm so glad you're okay! We were so worried—I'm sorry I couldn't stop her-"

"It's okay," I whisper, "I'll be alright."

"Thank the goddess," she murmurs. "Layla, he's gone!"

"Gone? Who?"

"My dad! We were chasing him, chasing them all, trying to catch them to turn over to the security officers, and then took off into the forest. So we followed, but my dad—I guess he took a wrong turn and fell into a ravine. He snapped his neck—one of the others went down to verify, and he's gone." Tears stream down her cheeks, and my heart lurches for her.

Even though he was terrible, he was still her father. I know she was caught in the middle.

"Amber, I'm sorry, are you okay?"

"Okay? Layla, I'm fucking amazing! Are you kidding? This is the best thing that could happen. Mom and I are finally free of him!" She laughs giddily, and relief washes through me.

"Great, then I'm glad. Is everyone else okay?" My whispery tone forces her to lower her voice.

"Yeah, we're all fine. Well, the other guys got away, but we know who they are, so we can make sure they never come back."

I nod. "Okay, that works."

The squeal of tires draws everyone's attention to the parking lot entrance, where a tiny blue Toyota comes screeching in sideways.

Roxanne throws open the door and runs toward me, brandishing the spelled silver knife and glaring around us for the threat.

"Where is she? I'll kill that bitch right now, witch or no witch!"

Derrek speaks up. "She's gone, escaped before I could catch her."

Roxanne's appraising gaze lands on Derrek, then she looks to me in question.

"He saved my life," I force out loud enough for her to hear.

She raises one eyebrow. "It seems a lot happened in the last hour besides a homecoming dance."

I emit a whispery giggle. "Just a little."

"Roxanne?" My uncle's voice is hesitant, unsure. He and a few of the other people that were meant to be attending a ball tonight stride out of the trees.

My beta's posture immediately stiffens, and she straightens herself to her full height. "If you think you can just come *waltzing* back here after disappearing in the middle of the night, you've got another think coming. You're not the alpha anymore and there's nothing to keep me from giving you a piece of my mind. You selfish, pompous, ass-"

Her angry speech is cut off when my uncle reaches her, wrapping his thick arms around her body and dragging her mouth to his. In a split second, she melts, her brown fingers stroking his pale cheeks as she kisses him back, and my heart flutters in my chest for her.

Abruptly, she pushes back. "Don't think that makes up for anything," she warns him with her sternest voice. "I'm still the beta and you are barely a member of this pack any more. I can issue you a command to scrub the toilets, or mow the lawn, or-"

"I'll do anything you say, my dearest," he purrs with a kiss to her cheek. "So long as you let me stay."

"Well, I mean," she replies, flustered. "That's really up to the alpha."

Uncle Dom's eyes turn in my direction, and he nods

solemnly. "I know I have a lot of explaining to do, Layla. I'd be grateful if you'd hear me out."

I stare at him for a minute, as if weighing my options. Then I answer, "Okay. But it's Lilliana."

Chapter Thirty

LAYLA

~

Naturally, the one big event the last two weeks were leading up to—the dance—is ruined. We all trudge into the beautifully decorated space, filthy, bedraggled, and weary, and the caterers stare in absolute shock. Roxanne speaks swiftly to the DJ, who puts on a mellow playlist akin to elevator music and disappears. Instead of rushing the dance floor, we pile into the chairs artfully arranged around a few tables. The caterers pop up more tables and chairs, and as other people arrive still beautifully dressed for the dance, they're filled in on the night's events.

The guys, Derrek, Roxanne, my uncle, and I have claimed a table, and that's when the entire story comes out.

The moment my uncle realized the curse had transferred from him to me, he booked it directly to Pack Montrose. Apparently, unbeknownst to anyone else, he's been secretly in contact with someone there for years. He, like I, was convinced there's more to the curse and our pack feud than they led us to believe. As alpha, there was very little he could do. Freed of that constraint, he set out to figure out a way to break the curse for good.

Dom blended in with Pack Montrose, under the guise of being a lone wolf, who left another pack further south. He got a job—in a hardware shop of all things—and kept to himself as much as possible, trying to work his connections and find the answer.

He was in town one day and saw Derrek, recognized him from LA. Shocked, he immediately yanked him into an alley and demanded to know what he was doing and what was going on back here. Derrek admitted everything, but also that he knew Azalea wanted to kill me and was keeping tabs on her. His plan was to be there when she eventually made her move.

They coordinated, and as I had never officially banished my uncle—this was apparently a thing I needed to learn to do—he could get them both into our pack territory, and follow Azalea.

"So wait, the pack territory is protected, right?" I ask, confused. "I thought that meant no one but pack can cross it?"

"Yes, and no. Anyone who has not been specifically banned can cross it without help. When they enacted the safeguards, they issued a blanket ban for any descendants of Derrek's great grandmother. That includes him and his cousin," Dom answers.

"So how were *both* of them able to get here, then?"

"I invited Derrek the first time, so that waved his ban. When Peter Jean-Yves invited Azalea, that negated the ancient ban."

"So if your invite allowed Derrek on the land, why did you need to help him on again?"

"You asked him to leave," Roxanne answers. "As the alpha, you told him to leave and never come back. That essentially re-issued the ban."

"Which, apparently *anyone* can break?"

"It's complicated," my uncle admits. "If you want to permanently ban someone in such a way that a member of the pack can't invite them, you have to word it specifically. Otherwise, it's pretty relaxed."

"I see." I think about for a long minute. My head is killing me, a feeling like static electricity pinging up my skull where Azalea had crushed my neck. "Well, I think we should get a list of the men who were with Peter Jean-Yves tonight, so I can issue them a permanent and complete ban. It was way too easy for them to smuggle Azalea onto the property. Oh, we need to ban her, too."

"On it," Roxanne nods, whipping out her phone and texting.

"I'd say it's a bit late for that," a deep voice announces, and as one, our pack turns to face the newcomer.

I don't recognize him; he looks about my uncle's

age, with more silver than dark hair, and he's burly—I finally understand the meaning of the word 'barrel-chested'. He's dressed in a wool coat with a button-down shirt and slacks, casual, nothing remarkable.

But his very presence sets my teeth on edge and sends my wolf snarling, clawing at my insides to be set free.

I'm immediately on my feet, striding forward to meet this new threat. He has two others with him, two others who, like him, don't belong here.

My pack surges in behind me; we far outnumber them. They have no hope of overpowering us, and I don't sense any of Azalea's witch magic in the air.

I pull myself up to my full height—a good foot shorter than this beast, but I have my mates at my back for confidence. "You don't belong here," I state, my voice deep and threatening.

The older man stares down at me with little interest. "You're correct, Harridan. I don't."

"You have no right to be on my lands."

"I'm only here to claim what's mine; we don't want trouble, and we'll leave peaceably. I promise you."

I can feel phantom hackles rise on my neck. When I speak, my alpha timbre reverberates in my chest. "Nothing here is yours to claim."

Around me, the pack rumbles their agreement.

"That, I'm afraid, is where you're mistaken."

"Who are you?"

"I'm Avery Nielsen." He says it like I should know what it means, but I've never heard that name.

"He's the alpha of Pack Montrose," Roxanne whispers from my right.

A snarl rumbles in my chest, echoed by the several hundred wolves in the room.

"And what is it you're here to claim?"

"My son."

Dom laughs. "If you've lost your kid, Nielsen, it's no business of ours. No one here is harboring a Pack Montrose runaway, are you?"

A chorus of voices confirm my uncle's assertion.

The other pack alpha just grins. "Oh, he's here. He just doesn't know where he belongs. But I'll show you. Do I have your permission to claim my blood, and leave without violence, Harridan?"

I turn the query over in my mind, but I can't see a downside. There's no wolf here that's from Pack Montrose, aside from the two he brought with him. If I word it correctly, I can give him permission and compel him to leave in one swift phrase.

My eyes dart to Roxanne, and she nods subtly.

Drawing in a deep breath, I face the beast of a man. "Very well; I give you permission to claim your child, if he's here, and leave, permanently." The double-timbre of my alpha voice reverberates through the room, sealing the magical command.

Nielsen grins, but it's more a flash of teeth than an actual smile. When he speaks, the dull hazel of his eyes glows, and I experience an alpha command from the other side for the first time since I learned about wolves. It doesn't compel me, but it tickles uncomfortably in my

319

ears. "Leaf Garrow, I claim you as my son and heir. Come, it's time to go home."

Panic erupts in my chest. "What? No, you can't just pick someone and claim them. A child is only by blood." My eyes dart back to Derrek, who looks just as shocked as I am, his face red.

Nielsen releases a loud, booming laugh. "Don't you get it, girl? That warlock abomination *is* my son. What-ever claim you may have on him, he belongs with me, and you've already given me permission to take him."

"No, I take it back! It's his choice!"

"It doesn't work that way, I'm afraid. No take-back-sies. Leaf! Come along, *now*." He uses his alpha voice again, and I cringe at the way he speaks to Derrek like a dog.

Derrek steps awkwardly toward the bigger man, his steps dragging as he tries, and fails, to fight the command.

My hands whip out, clutching Derrek's fingers, and I try to pull on him even as he's ripped away.

"Thanks for the hospitality, Harridan. Looks like a hell of a party," Nielsen snorts. "Come along, son." He wraps an arm around Derrek's shoulders and the younger man visibly cringes.

All eyes turn to me, shocked that I'm allowing them to leave, but what else can I do?

Roxanne sends a swift text, then leans over. "I'm sending our security to make sure they leave pack lands and hopefully catch whoever enabled them to cross. Likely it was one of Jen-Yves's cronies."

I nod, numb, and watch Derrek's back as they walk through the ornate hallway toward the front door. Before they pass through, he turns to gaze at me one last time, his eyes flashing bright green beneath the mop of curls, and he gives me the saddest smile before he disappears into the night.

Several pack members take it upon themselves to follow the intruders out. I'm frozen, my feet rooted to the spot, and all the surrounding noise as people express their shock and anger turns into a vague hum in my ears.

Because all I know right now is the painful splintering in my chest.

In that brief moment when our fingers touched, I finally knew it. I felt the same electric tingles warm my skin, running all the way to my core.

And when I allowed the Montrose Alpha to take him away, those tingles became knives shredding at my heart.

Derrek is my mate. My *fourth* fated mate.

And I just let him slip away.

The End

Ready for the epic conclusion of The Midnight Wolves of Smoky Falls trilogy? The story continues in Dawn of the Pack

Let's be friends!

THANK you so much for reading my books, it truly means the world to me that I can share these crazy ideas with you.

If you'd like to stay apprised of my upcoming projects (there are so many!) Please join my bi-weekly newsletter. You'll get exclusive sneak peeks and chances to win goodies that are only offered to my subscribers—plus you'll have the opportunity to download more of my work free right away!

So what are you waiting for?

Join my newsletter now!
http://laurelnight.com/newsletter

Also by Laurel Night

THE WARRIOR QUEEN LEGACY - COMPLETE SERIES

A **SLOW-BURN REVERSE** harem romance featuring a fantasy dystopian setting that has been compared to 'I Am Legend' crossed with 'The Shanarra Chronicles' and wolf shifters. Named one of Book Authority's Top Fantasy Books of 2021, and Red Feather Romance's 10 Top Adult Fantasy Romances. Available on Amazon and more.

SCENT OF DECEPTION - A STANDALONE IN THE BONDS OF STEELE OMEGAVERSE

Raised to be a pampered omega, Sapphire Steele never manifested. Desperate, she accepted a lucrative proposal: Pretend to be the omega for a wealthy pack until one of the alphas receives his inheritance, then disappear with her share of the money…. But someone knows her secret… Available on Amazon and more

GLAM - A STANDALONE MAFIA-LITE REVERSE HAREM ROMANCE

The hardworking daughter of two cops finally lands her dream job, only to be interrupted on her first day by three devastatingly handsome mafia brothers she recognized from college. Always out of her reach before, they're suddenly obsessed with her, and insist she become a part of their glittering world. Then, one night she witnesses first hand what happens in the back room of those shimmering parties, and how the Vargas family have ruled over Miami for decades.

Terrified, she knows with certainty that one of two things will happen: Either she becomes theirs, beholden to them and immersed in their world of wealth and privilege for the rest of her life.

Or no one will ever hear from her again. Check it out on Amazon

About the Author

LAUREL NIGHT IS a long-time fan of romance and adventure. She's traveled the world, and currently resides in the shadow of the Great Smoky Mountains with her daughter Tessa.

For more about Laurel, her books, and future projects, you can find her at www.laurelnight.com, or hanging around in Laurel's Night Queens, her group on Facebook.

If you'd like to stay up to date on Laurel's work, you can join Laurel's newsletter.